LONELY IS THE GUNFIGHTER

Morgan 'Coop' Cooper is a man with a tragic past and an uncertain future. Drifting into the town of Rocas Rojas, his trail crosses with that of enigmatic saloon owner Lorna Rutledge. They hit it off immediately — but there is more to Lorna than meets the eye. Almost before he knows it, Coop finds himself teamed up with a gunman named Gospel Curtis, and robbing a gold train at Deep River Gorge . . .

STEVE HAYES

LONELY IS THE GUNFIGHTER

Complete and Unabridged

LINFORD
Leicester

First published in Great Britain in 2017

First Linford Edition
published 2018

A catalogue record for this book is available
from the British Library.

ISBN 978–1–4448–3557–1

Published by
F. A. Thorpe (Publishing)
Anstey, Leicestershire

Set by Words & Graphics Ltd.
Anstey, Leicestershire
Printed and bound in Great Britain by
T. J. International Ltd., Padstow, Cornwall

This book is printed on acid-free paper

Prologue

Neither gunman seemed aware of the other.

Shirtless, they stood back-to-back, one facing east, the other west, digging in tight-lipped silence. Both men wore shabby sun-faded jeans, scuffed boots and Stetsons that were soiled from years of use. Equally old and worn were their gunbelts and tied-down, quick-draw holsters, but not the revolvers tucked in them. Knowing their lives depended on their six-shooters, the gunmen kept them well-oiled and in perfect condition.

In grim unison each man dug his long-handled shovel into the red clay-like ground, tamped it down with his boot, swung it up and heaved the shovelful of dirt over his shoulder. It landed on the dirt already piled around the edge of the grave.

Overhead the noonday desert sun

was blistering hot.

Neither gunman said a word.

Occasionally, one or both men stopped digging long enough to spit the dust from his mouth and to drink from his canteen. But they never looked at each other or acknowledged one another in any way. They just stood there, staring straight ahead, expressions devoid of emotion, eyes as blank and empty as any corpse. Then, once their thirst was temporarily quenched, each gunman grabbed his bandana, wiped the sweat from his face and continued digging.

They dug until mid-afternoon. By then the grave was seven feet long, five feet wide and four feet deep, and both gunmen were soaked in sweat. As if on a silent signal they agreed that the grave was now big enough and stopped digging. Both leaned their shovels against the wall, took a final swig of water and then poured the rest over their bare heads.

Two Morgan silver dollars fell out of the taller man's canteen. He wasn't surprised. He'd dropped them into it

before making the long ride across the desert in order to preserve the water. It was an old trick that he'd learned from a grizzled prospector in Death Valley, California, and he'd used it ever since. Picking up the coins, he stuffed them into his pocket then tossed his canteen onto the dirt now piled high above them and faced the other man.

''Fore we go any farther, I want to make something clear.'

'What?'

'You don't have to do this, mister. I'm willing to say you're faster than me and go on my way.'

The shorter gunman gave an ugly laugh. 'Not a chance.'

'Okay. Suit yourself.'

'I intend to, you smug bastard. Now, quit yapping and let's get to the meat.'

The taller gunman sighed, resigned to the fact that he couldn't escape another killing.

'How you want to call it?' he asked.

'On three suit you?'

'Sure. Who's going to count?'

'Makes no matter to me.'

'You, then.'

'Agreed,' said the shorter gunman.

Both men stepped back as far as the end wall of the grave would let him, faced his opponent and prepared to draw.

'Ready?'

'Ready.'

'One. Two . . . Three!'

Their six-shooters cleared leather almost simultaneously, the booms of the two shots so close they sounded as one.

But only the tall gunman, Morgan 'Coop' Cooper remained standing.

The shorter gunman crumpled to the ground, his Colt .45 still clutched in his hand, blood pumping from a fatal bullet hole in his chest.

Coop holstered his gun, a Dance Brothers .44, single-action, six-shot revolver with an 8-inch barrel, brass trigger guard and walnut grips that his father had used while fighting for the Confederacy during the Civil War. He looked down at the dead man, feeling no remorse for him. He didn't know him or even know his name. He was just another nameless fast gun trying to enhance his reputation by killing a notorious gunfighter. He'd failed, like all the others before him, and paid the ultimate price.

And that should have been the end of it.

But as Coop looked at the blood-stained corpse, he knew it wasn't. It was just the beginning and he gave a regretful sigh. He derived no pleasure from killing another man, but at the same time he sure as hell wasn't going to lose any sleep over it. Kill or be killed was the gunman's creed and long ago Coop had resigned himself to the probability that he would not live long enough to witness any change.

Perhaps worse, he knew that he'd never forget the dead man. Now his face would join the gallery of other gunmen he'd killed — faces that haunted his dreams nightly, turning them into nightmares — and that was damned frustrating.

Equally frustrating was the fact that there was nothing Coop could do about it. Well, almost nothing. There was one way he could get relief, if only temporary. He tried to dismiss the temptation, but it was too late. Once he'd thought of it, it only grew stronger and stronger until finally he couldn't resist it. He grabbed his shovel, dug a toe-hold in the side-wall, grasped the edge of the grave and pulled himself out.

Nearby, two saddled horses were tied to a clump of mesquite. One of them was a rangy, long-legged buckskin with a cropped mane; the other a small, sturdy red roan.

Coop walked to the buckskin, pulled a half-empty bottle of cheap whiskey from the saddlebag and took a long drink. The rotgut burned all the way down. He grimaced, gulped in some air and then drained the bottle. This time the alcohol burned his throat so badly for several seconds he couldn't breathe. Goddammit, he thought. *No wonder the Indians call it firewater!*

But there was no denying the whiskey was doing its job. Already Coop felt less frustrated, less depressed and somewhat mellow. He also felt charitable, which was a rarity and turning to the buckskin, gently rubbed its velvety-soft nose.

The horse, unaccustomed to affection, pulled its head back and suspiciously bared its teeth.

The buckskin's reaction had a sobering effect on Coop. It snapped him back to reality and he jerked his hand away before the horse could bite him. He then cursed the ornery animal and went to untie the reins.

It was then he realized he was still holding the empty whiskey bottle in his other hand. He scowled at it as if it were his enemy and tried to assure himself that he wasn't relying on whiskey more and more these days to silence the guilt he felt after each killing. But deep down, where the truth lives in every man, Coop knew he was deluding himself. Unlike his early years as a gunfighter, when shooting another gunman never troubled him, now, knowing he was responsible for a man's death — even a man intent on killing him — gnawed at his conscience and made him feel guilty.

He couldn't remember exactly when the guilt had started, but he knew it had been building over the last few years and he found it unsettling. It meant his conscience, which he'd successfully kept buried since the death of his wife, Helen, was trying to resurface . . . and that was something he couldn't allow.

A conscience was the last thing he or any gunfighter needed and Coop had ignored it at first, hoping it would go away. But it didn't. With each shooting it only got worse until lately it was with him constantly and hard as he tried, he could no longer ignore it. Not sober anyway.

That's when he'd turned to the bottle. The whiskey didn't remove his guilt but it did deaden his mind so that he could tolerate the emotional pain it caused. The trouble was, eventually the 'cure' became a new problem — just as it had before when he'd first used whiskey to help him get over the sudden death of his beloved wife. He'd finally licked that, but now his craving had returned. Worse, as each day passed, it took more and more whiskey to bury his guilt . . . until finally he was drinking so much it hampered his reflexes, making him vulnerable to any upstart gunman whom he could easily out-draw when sober.

The answer, Coop knew, was simple: quit drinking or at least limit the amount so that he never lost his edge. A year ago that wouldn't have been a problem. But now that whiskey had gotten its hooks into him, he knew it would be a battle. In fact, as he looked at the empty bottle he realized that so long as he kept killing, staying sober might be the hardest thing he'd ever had to do — with the exception of the day he buried Helen.

But it had to be done and it had to be done now.

With that in mind Coop went to throw the bottle away. As he did, he saw there were a few drops of whiskey left inside. He tried to ignore them. But unable to stop himself, he held the bottle to his lips and savored each drop as it trickled over his tongue. Then, angry at himself for succumbing to the temptation, he threw the empty bottle off into the sunbaked desert, returned to the grave, grabbed his shovel and began covering the dead gunfighter with dirt.

1

It had just stopped raining when Coop rode into Rocas Rojas, a lawless, grubby little eyesore on the U.S. side of the New Mexico-Mexican border. Named for the giant red rocks that dotted the otherwise bleak landscape, the town consisted of a shabby hotel, an old adobe mission, a few clapboard shacks, telegraph office, grim-looking bank with iron-barred windows, Henson's livery stable, and two saloons that doubled as brothels and were always filled with border riffraff.

Though it was only mid-morning, Coop reined up before the first saloon he came to — a battered, two-story adobe relic known as Holy Moses, or *Moises Santos* as the Mexicans called it. Dismounting, he tied the horses to the hitch-rail and grabbed his saddle-bags and carbine. There was no boardwalk on either side of the street, only ankle-deep mud. Worse, the mud was saturated with foul-smelling horses' urine and piles of dung and Coop was careful where he stepped as he approached the entrance.

As he walked, he pushed his slicker back and with his thumb unhooked the strap securing his six-shooter in the holster. He wasn't expecting trouble, but that didn't mean it wasn't waiting for him inside. It often was and the only reason he was still alive was because he always prepared for it. Today was no different. He paused as he reached the old sagging door, took a deep calming breath, exhaled slowly and then cautiously pushed it open.

Once inside, Coop paused and looked around. It was a familiar sight, no different than all the other tacky saloons he'd been in throughout the west. The long bar facing him was crowded with loud boisterous drinkers — prospectors, miners, carpetbaggers, drifters or cowboys still grimy with trail dirt. Coop looked them over. Satisfied that none of them posed a threat, he then checked out the poker players. At each of the gaming tables sat a slick-haired, well-dressed gambler deftly dealing Faro or five-card stud to the same type of eager drunks at the bar.

No threat there, either.

Lastly, Coop's gaze settled on the piano player. Pushing fifty, he was a small insignificant-looking man who looked even smaller and more insignificant in a black threadbare preacher's coat that was too big for him. The rest of his attire was just as ill-fitting and shabby. His gray pin-striped pants needed pressing, his white shirt had beer stains on it and his shoes needed polishing. The soiled, poorly-tied bowtie and the battered bowler perched atop his head added to his rundown appearance, as did his straggly graying black hair, unkempt beard and the old frayed cushion that he had to sit on in order to reach the keys of the dilapidated upright piano. Additionally, he wasn't much of a pianist and was desperately trying to make up for it by playing as loudly as he could. Strangely though, despite all these detriments, there was something likeable about him and the beer glass sitting on top of the piano overflowed with tips.

Coop, deciding he was harmless, continued to look around the saloon. His gaze settled on one of the many rouge-cheeked, heavily powdered bargirls whose bulging fleshy bodies were stuffed into tight-fitting colorful dresses. None of them were pretty, but it didn't matter. They were *women*, a rare commodity in small towns and gold camps throughout the Southwest, and they had no trouble persuading the customers to buy them watered-down drinks or to accompany them upstairs to one of the bedrooms.

Coop gave them a quick once-over. None of them looked familiar or troublesome. Dismissing them, he bulled his way through the jostling crowd, right hand on the butt of his six-shooter, ready to draw if provoked. But no old enemies or the relatives of someone he'd killed confronted him and he reached the crowded bar without incident. There was no room for him, so he elbowed aside two drunks arguing at one end, set his carbine and saddlebags on the bar and ordered a beer from the taller of the two white-aproned, mustachioed bartenders.

'Cost you a cartwheel, mister.'

'That's a mighty stiff price.'

'Take it up with management.'

Coop was too thirsty to argue. He tossed the tall bartender a silver dollar and took a long satisfying gulp of warm frothy beer. It quenched his thirst and, better yet, had less of a hold on him compared to whiskey. As he set the glass down and wiped his mouth on his sleeve, a voluptuous, brassy blond with hard brittle eyes as blue as her skimpy dress approached and asked him to buy her a drink.

Never a womanizer, he didn't bother to look at her or even answer.

She asked him again, this time

rubbing her big powdered breasts against him.

Hoping to end her pestering, he growled: 'When hell freezes over!'

Immune to insults, she said cheerfully: 'Name's Dulcie, honey. What's yours?'

Again, Coop didn't answer.

'What's the matter, cowboy? You sore about something?'

Coop continued to ignore her.

'Is it your gal?' Dulcie pressed. 'Did she run off? Is that what you're sore about?'

'I don't have a girl,' Coop replied grimly.

'What about your wife?' Dulcie asked, noticing the thin circle of pale skin on the ring finger of his left hand. 'Don't she count?'

About to tell her to go to hell, Coop heard honest concern in her voice. Curious, he turned and looked at her. All the brittleness in her china-blue eyes had disappeared, replaced by a genuine empathy that made him feel obliged to answer her.

'I don't have a wife, neither.'

'I figured as much. But you did once, right?'

'Once,' he grudgingly admitted. 'Now she's in a better place.'

'Amen,' said Dulcie. 'I lost my kid brother last year, so I know how much it hurts.'

'There's no pain like it.'

'Is that why you took off your wedding ring — so it wouldn't remind you of her?'

'Something like that.'

'Makes sense,' Dulcie said, understanding. 'Me, I burned everything belonging to Timmy and hopped on the first train out here, figuring the farther I got from St. Louis, the less it would hurt.'

'How'd that turn out?'

'It didn't. I still miss him every minute of every day and guess I always will.' She sighed regretfully then swallowed her pain and brightened. 'You know, cowboy, maybe we could help each other.'

'I doubt it.'

'It's worth a try, ain't it?'

Coop didn't answer.

'What do you got to lose? I mean, even a fine-looking gent like you needs to chase the rabbit now and then. And if you was to come upstairs with me, we could comfort each other and maybe forget our pain for a while — ' She stopped, startled, as someone grabbed her from behind and spun her around.

'What the hell — ?' she exclaimed angrily and then broke off in alarm as she saw who'd grabbed her.

2

'F-Foley,' Dulcie stammered. 'I'm sorry. I didn't know it was you.'

'Beat it,' snarled Ezra Foley, ''fore I sell your no-good fat ass to the Comanches!'

Dulcie cringed fearfully, 'Sure, sure,' and scurried off.

The small, rat-faced, black-clad gunman turned to Coop. 'Hey, you!'

Coop ignored him.

Foley grabbed Coop's arm and jerked him away from the bar. 'Goddammit, mister, look at me when I'm talking to you!'

Coop barely seemed to move. But his sudden back-handed blow across Foley's face slammed the little man into the two hardened gunmen standing behind him.

'Keep your goddam hands off me,' Coop warned, 'or jerk that iron!'

Foley started to draw. Then he saw the deadliness in Coop's flint-gray eyes and changed his mind. But not wanting to look cowardly before his men or the onlookers gathered around them, he puffed up like a belligerent rooster and crowed: 'Forget it, mister! You ain't prodding me into slapping leather. I got bigger plans for you!'

Coop laughed contemptuously, 'The cheaper the gunman, the cheaper the threat,' and went on drinking his beer.

Foley whitened with fury. 'Go ahead! Laugh, you damn drifter! You won't find it so funny when we march you outside and stretch your goddamned neck!'

'On what charge — or ain't you trumped one up yet?'

'Murder!'

'Careful, sonny. Murder's not something to joke about.'

'I ain't joking! You gunned down Joe Holly and you're going to swing for it.'

'You got the wrong man,' Coop said. 'I don't know anyone named Joe Holly.'

'That didn't stop you from shooting

him in the back!'

'You must be hard of hearing, sonny. I just said I don't know any Joe Hollys.'

'Then how come you got Joe's horse tied up outside?'

'Which horse might that be?'

'The red roan,' broke in the younger of the two gunmen, Ned Crouch. 'Joe raised that horse from a wet-nosed colt, and the only way you could've gotten your hands on it is by back-shooting him.'

'I never back-shot anyone in my life,' Coop said. 'And even if the fella I killed was Joe Holly, he brought it on himself.'

'Oh, yeah? How?'

'By forcing a showdown. I gave him a way out, but he wouldn't take it. Hell, he even insisted on this crazy notion about digging a grave for the loser. I figured he was *loco*, but I went along anyway, hoping I could talk him out of it. But I couldn't. He was dead set on adding another notch to his gun and there was nothing I could do to change his mind.'

'That sounds like Joe, all right,' the older gunman, Val Wallace admitted. 'He's one stubborn sonofabitch!'

'And now, thanks to you,' Crouch told Coop, 'he's a *dead* sonofabitch.'

'Man's got a right to defend himself.'

'That don't include shooting Joe in the back,' said Foley, 'or stealing his horse.'

Coop sighed wearily. 'Jesus, mister, how many times do I got to tell you? I didn't shoot your pal in the back.'

'And I say you're a goddamn liar!'

Instantly, the whole bar went quiet.

Coop smiled — a chilling smile that would have frightened a ghost.

'Liar?' he repeated softly. 'Now that's one word I truly won't tolerate.'

No one saw him move, but suddenly his six-shooter was pressed under Foley's chin.

Foley froze — eyes bright with fear as he knew he was a trigger-squeeze from death.

Crouch came to his rescue. 'Hold it, mister,' he told Coop. 'No reason to drop that hammer on 'count of jackass talk.'

''Jackass talk'?'

'Sure. When Foley, here, gets to drinking, he talks like a goddamned jackass.'

'That's true, mister,' Wallace added. 'Swear to God! Couple of drinks and just about anything's likely to come out of his mouth. And most of it stupid.'

'Maybe so,' Coop said grimly. 'But that don't excuse him for calling me a liar.'

''Course it don't. Man calls you a liar, most cases you got a right to brace him on it.'

'Then how come you're butting in?'

'Because Foley, he ain't most cases. I mean, sure, the dumb bastard called you a liar. We all heard him. But that ain't what he meant — '

'That's right,' broke in Crouch. 'What he meant was — there ain't a man living who could gun down Joe. 'Least, not face-on.'

'I did,' Coop said quietly. 'What's

more, I'll tell you where he's buried. Then you can go dig the sonofabitch up and see that he was shot in the chest, not the back.'

That seemed to satisfy Crouch and Wallace, but not Foley.

'What the hell you two bone-heads waiting for?' he yelled at them. 'Throw a rope over the bastard and haul his lying ass outside!'

'Hold it!'

3

The voice came from the second floor. It was a sensual, cultured voice made all the more alluring by a refined English accent.

Coop, and everyone else, looked up at the tall graceful woman standing at the top of the stairs leading to the second floor. She was an eyeful. In her early thirties, her long sun-colored hair was pulled back in a shimmering bun, diamonds glittered about her neck and she looked elegantly stunning in a gold lame gown that reached to the floor.

'What the devil's going on down there?' she demanded, glaring at Foley.

Though intimidated, he tried to hide it as he said: 'N-Nothing.'

'Don't give me that nonsense! I asked you a question, Foley. Answer it!'

'Dammit, this ain't none of your business, Miss — '

The woman cut Foley off. 'Everything that *happens* in this bloody saloon is my business, you mindless little toad!'

Foley flinched and angrily gritted his teeth.

'And if you wish to dispute that,' she continued, 'then I suggest you take it up with Curtis.' She smiled smugly and glanced at one of the closed bedroom doors. 'That's if you got the nerve to disturb him right now.'

Foley licked his lips but said nothing.

'I thought not,' the woman mocked. 'Like Curtis says: you're gutless to the core!'

Furious, Foley started to draw. But even as his hand touched the butt of his gun, his nerve failed him and he couldn't go through with it.

'Well, what're you waiting for, shorty?' the woman taunted. 'Go ahead! Shoot me!'

The saloon went quiet. Everyone, including Coop and the drunks at the bar, stared at Foley, waiting to see what he'd do next.

He did nothing — except quiver with rage.

The woman leaned on the handrail, looked down at the crowd and gave a scornful shrug. 'I'm sorry, ladies and gentlemen, but it appears that Mr. Foley is too bloody yellow to back up his mealy-mouthed threats!'

Everyone laughed.

Humiliated, Foley seemed to shrink even smaller than he already was.

The woman chose this moment to slowly descend the stairs. Every step, every calculated movement reflected a strange mix of bawdiness and regal sensuality.

She took her time, enjoying the drama, and on reaching the bottom of the stairs brushed past Foley as if he didn't exist and confronted Coop.

'At the risk of being presumptuous, cowboy, can I buy you a drink?'

Coop, glad to avoid another gunfight, nodded. 'Sure.'

'Then kindly follow me.'

She led him to a corner table that

was occupied by a gaunt veteran dealer and four grimy miners playing cut-throat poker.

'Gents,' she said to them, 'I wonder if you'd mind finding another table.'

The five men minded all right, but they knew better than to argue. With forced smiles, they picked up their money and hurried away.

Coop laid his carbine and saddlebags on the table and pulled out the woman's chair.

'I knew it,' she purred. 'Knew it the moment I laid eyes on you.'

'Knew what?'

'You were a gentleman.'

'If I am,' Coop said wryly, 'you're the first person to mention it.'

The woman laughed. It was a soft lyrical laugh that reminded him of a similar laugh, one he'd once enjoyed every day but would never hear again, and momentarily he had trouble burying the memory of his dead wife.

'Well,' the woman said, mistaking his silence, 'I'm obviously not going to win you over with flattery.'

'Don't mean you should stop trying,' Coop said.

'I don't intend to, cowboy. I know a good catch when I see it.'

Normally her boldness would have chased him away. He disliked pushy women and usually ignored them until they gave up on him and left. But for some odd reason he found himself not only interested in this alluring woman, but enjoying her company.

'Then all I can say, ma'am, is you need spectacles.'

She laughed again. 'Modest, too! I admire that in a man. Shows he's got nothing to prove — ' She paused as the short bartender approached. Coop hadn't seen her signal to him, but he was carrying a tray holding two shot glasses and a bottle of bourbon. Thanking him, she waited until he'd left then poured their drinks and raised her glass in toast to Coop: 'To new friendships.'

'And long-lasting ones,' he said, clinking glasses with her.

They drank.

The expensive, aged bourbon went down smoother than melted honey. It left hints of vanilla and caramel in Coop's mouth and he raised his eyebrows in appreciation.

'To your liking?' the woman asked, pouring him another.

'You keep serving me bourbon like this,' he said, savoring the taste, 'and you'll have trouble getting rid of me.'

'Who says I want to? Frankly, I'm delighted to meet a man who doesn't have dirt under his fingernails or tobacco juice dribbling down his chin, but instead has manners and enjoys the finer things in life. Am I not right?' she added when he didn't respond.

Coop foolishly let his mind wander. 'There was a time,' he admitted wistfully, 'before the war, when Helen was still alive, that we enjoyed a more elegant lifestyle and . . . ' He stopped as the memories of his late wife became too painful to endure.

The woman seemed to understand

his pain. 'My intuition was right about you.'

'Meaning?'

'You *don't* belong in here.'

'I'll take that as a compliment, ma'am.'

'That's how I meant it. And it's miss, not ma'am.'

'Miss, what?'

'Rutledge. Lorna Rutledge. And you?'

'Morgan Cooper.'

Her eyebrows arched in surprise. 'Well, well,' she said, impressed. 'May I say, Mr. Cooper, it's an honor to have a man of your vaunted reputation in my establishment.'

'Save the bee-sweetening for your flapjacks, Miss Rutledge.'

'Oh, that's right. I forgot. You dislike flattery. Well, bee-sweetening aside, there's something I need to ask — '

'No, I didn't,' Coop interrupted. 'I gunned Joe Holly down face-on, just like I told your men back there.'

'*My* men?' Lorna gave a scornful

laugh. 'Good Lord, that trash doesn't belong to me, Mr. Cooper.'

'Call me Coop.'

'Only if you'll call me Lorna.'

'Be my pleasure.'

'I'm flattered.'

'You're also dangerous.'

'Dangerous?' Lorna laughed. 'Why on earth would you ever think that?'

Coop wearily rolled his eyes. 'Please, Miss Lorna, don't act coy with me.'

'Me? Coy?'

'And don't act shocked, either. It ain't your style.'

'Oh? What is my style?'

'Rotgut, beer and sawdust floors.'

'Ouch.'

'No offense meant.'

'None taken, *Mister* Cooper.'

'Coop, remember?'

'Ah yes, Coop,' Lorna said. 'Forgive me, but it's such a hard name to pronounce.'

He knew she was toying with him and refused to take the bait.

'Well?' Lorna prodded. 'I'm waiting, Coop?'

'For what?'

'A moment ago you told me not to act coy. Or shocked. So, how *should* I act?'

'Might try being yourself.'

'You mean . . . quit acting like Queen Victoria and lay my cards on the table?'

'Something like that.'

'Very well. But I'd like to see your cards first.'

'Fair enough. Why did you — ?'

'Interfere?'

'Yeah. You don't know me. So why go out on a limb to save my neck?'

'Let's just say I didn't want that miserable little runt to kill you.'

'Or me to kill him?'

'You serious?' Lorna laughed in disgust. 'Why, I'd happily pay for the coffin if I knew Foley would be in it!'

'Judas,' Coop said, surprised by her venom. 'Remind me not to get you riled at me.'

'That could never happen.'

'Lucky me.'

'Luck has nothing to do with it,

cowboy. First time I saw you lightning struck.'

'Now *I'm* flattered.'

'What's more,' Lorna said as if Coop hadn't spoken, 'I knew instantly I'd be a fool if I let a man like you walk out of my life without meeting you.'

'And now that we've met? What's the verdict?'

'A royal flush.'

'No bee-sweetening, remember?'

Lorna laughed. 'Sorry. Old habits, you know.'

Coop wanted to believe her, but instinct warned him not to. 'Okay, here's another question: You said I don't belong here. How about you?'

'What's an Englishwoman doing owning a saloon, you mean?

'Yeah.'

'That's a secret. And ladies never reveal their secrets.'

'Make an exception.'

'Fortunately,' she laughed, 'I don't have to. I'm no lady.'

'Now I'm even more curious.'

'You're also greedy, you know that?'

'Only when I find a woman worth knowing.'

'How gallant!' She reached for the bottle to refill his glass, but he shook his head.

'Two's my limit.'

She looked surprised and mildly suspicious. 'My daddy told me to never trust a man who can't hold his liquor.'

'*My* daddy told me to never trust *anyone* — drunk or sober.'

'Trumped again,' Lorna said, amused. She downed her bourbon before adding: 'Actually, you're the first person I've met that I wouldn't mind telling my past to. I should warn you however, it's not pretty.'

'Then forget I asked.'

'Not a chance. Lightning seldom strikes twice and I don't want to lose you because I — ' She paused as a fight between two drunken miners broke out. One man wildly swung at the other, missed, and almost fell. His opponent staggered forward, fists wildly swinging, and the two ended up grappling and cursing each other.

'No, no, let the bartenders handle it,' Lorna said as Coop reached for his carbine. 'This dump needs repainting, anyway.'

Coop chuckled. 'Practical as well as beautiful!'

'Now who's bee-sweetening?'

'Sorry.'

'I forgive you — on one condition. You escort me home. No,' she added as he looked up at the gallery, 'that's my office. Home is across the street.'

'Fair enough,' Coop said. He helped Lorna up, grabbed his carbine and saddlebags and accompanied her to the exit.

4

Once they were outside, Lorna smiled invitingly at him. 'How do you feel about chivalry, Mr. Cooper?'

'I ain't had much practice at it of late.'

'Then let me refresh your memory . . . ' She draped her arms about his neck and made it clear that she wanted him to pick her up.

He did, using his free arm, asking: 'Where to?'

'There,' she pointed across the street at a recently-built log house.

'Convenient.'

'That's why I had it built there.' She waited until he'd carried her halfway across the muddy street before adding: 'With lumber so expensive these days, it cost me a fortune. But it was worth it. Now, when I feel like relaxing, I don't have to be cooped up in a dump of a hotel room. I can just cross the street and — Oh-h!' She gave a startled gasp as he slipped in the mud and almost lost his balance.

'Don't worry,' Coop said. 'I ain't going to drop you.'

'You better not, cowboy. Not if you want to enjoy my good bourbon again!'

Coop chuckled. Then carefully avoiding all the muddy potholes and wagon ruts, he safely reached the house and set Lorna down on the porch step.

Thanking him, she took a key from her coat pocket and unlocked the front door. 'Before you come in,' she said, 'would you mind kicking off that mud.'

'Be happy to,' Coop said. ' — next time.'

'Next time?'

'I still got to bed down my horses.'

'Now?'

'Unless you got a reason I shouldn't?'

'Apparently,' Lorna said, irked, 'I'm not the only one who needs spectacles.'

'Meaning?'

'You obviously can't see past your

nose, cowboy, or you would've seen me throwing myself at you. I mean, what's a girl got to do to get you between her sheets?'

'Damned if I know,' Coop said wryly. 'But you're right about one thing. You sure 'ain't no lady!'

'Lucky you,' Lorna said, and dragged him into the house.

5

Afterward, they lay on her bed, chests heaving, sweaty bodies touching, eyes fixed on the ceiling, listening to the mosquitoes whining outside in the sweltering heat.

'If we're going to keep this up,' Lorna said, looking at the bare window, 'I need to buy curtains.'

'From where?' Coop asked. 'I didn't see a dry-goods store when I rode in.'

'That's because there isn't one. Everybody has to send away for things, which takes weeks. In fact if I was going to stay here, which I'm not, a dry-goods store would be a good investment.'

Coop frowned. 'You ain't staying?'

'Uh-uh. Soon as I sell the Holy Moses, I'm on the first train out of town.'

'To where?'

'I haven't decided yet. But I didn't

cross the Atlantic or put up with the heat, flies and wagon-blisters just to own a rundown saloon and brothel!'

'Seems like you're doing okay.'

'I'm trying.'

'Everybody tries. You succeed.'

'Now you're giving *me* more credit than I deserve,' Lorna said.

'Quit acting modest,' Coop grumbled. 'That don't suit you, either.'

'Okay. On one condition: you remove your spurs before they rip up my bed.'

'My spurs?' He glanced down and realized that in his lust for her he hadn't kicked off his jeans, boots or spurs. 'Well, that's a first,' he said.

'Careful,' Lorna teased. 'That sounds suspiciously like a compliment.'

Coop grinned, pulled up his jeans and removed his spurs. Then sitting on the edge of the bed, he took the makings from his shirt pocket, rolled himself a smoke and lit up. 'Would I be wearing out my welcome if I sat here for a spell?'

'I'll shoot you if you don't.'

'No need to be bashful about it.'

Lorna laughed. 'Bashful is something I've never been accused of. Besides, you can't leave. You haven't heard the story of my sordid life yet.'

'I got the impression you didn't want me to.'

'I do and I don't,' Lorna said. 'On one hand I'm afraid if I tell you the truth, I'll lose you and on the other, I won't be able to live with myself if I don't. Oh, what the hell?' she added. 'I've got nothing to lose. You'll be leaving in the morning anyway.'

'Possible.'

Lorna sighed regretfully. 'Okay, first thing you should know is I'm not English.'

'But your accent?'

'Phony. I'm as American as Kansas.'

'I don't get it,' Coop said. 'Why pretend you're English if — ?'

'Because this rich snooty family in Philadelphia insisted they wanted a *British* nanny to look after their kids. Anyway, I got the job. I worked long hours but I loved it. And the Finches treated me as if I were family — almost like their daughter, in fact.'

'So why'd you leave?'

'I had no choice. Their butler, Colton, raped me. And when I threatened to tell the Finches, he swore he'd kill me. So I left. After that, I tried to find work but without references, no one would hire me. The only way I could support myself was to . . . to . . . '

'You don't have to go on,' Coop said as Lorna paused.

'I want to. I don't know why — I've never wanted to tell anyone before — but now I want to. Besides, you can pretty much guess the rest anyway. I began whoring down by the docks, near the Fifth Ward. I figured it would only be temporary, but after a year or so the truth sank in and I realized that this was where I was going to end up.

'But then one night this elegant coach pulled up and the driver told me to get in. I was broke and hungry, so I did. Inside was this old white-haired gent who offered to pay me to go home with him. He said his wife had died a few years ago and until recently all he'd done was mourn her loss. But now, he'd finally gotten his grief under control and once more enjoyed the company of women. I must've looked uneasy because he added that he was too old to have sex and only wanted a companion.

'I was afraid at first and was going to turn him down. But, like I said, I was broke and hungry and besides, he looked harmless, so I agreed. Turned out to be the best decision I ever made. He treated me well and before I knew it a year had passed. Then, on New Year's Eve his heart gave out. By then I truly liked him and was sad to see him die. I was also upset because I thought I'd have to start whoring again. But his lawyer said that Mr. Miles had left me money in his will. It wasn't a lot, but it was enough for me to come out here and start life over as a saloonkeeper. Since then, I've never looked back.

Thanks to the Holy Moses, I'm making money hand over fist.'

'You're lucky,' Coop said. 'It ain't often a person finds a rainbow.'

'Or the pot of gold at the end of it,' Lorna said. 'And believe me, cowboy, I need that pot of gold if I'm ever going to get my daughter back.'

'You have a daughter?' Coop said, surprised.

'Yes. But thanks to this judge, who claimed I wasn't a fit mother, my ex-husband has custody of her right now. But soon that's all going to change. After I sell the Holy Moses, I'm going back to court and prove to the judge that although I'm not as rich as my ex-husband or own a big ranch like he does, I've got enough money to look after my child.' She paused to rein in her emotions before adding: 'But that's enough about me. How about you, Coop? What's your goal?'

'I'm living it.'

'Drifting?' she said, disappointed. 'That's not much of a goal.'

'Suits me.'

'Then I misjudged you. I thought for sure you'd want a ranch some place where you could raise cattle and have a wife and young'uns around you.'

'There are worse goals, I reckon.'

'But you'd sooner drift?'

Coop shrugged noncommittally. He'd started drifting when his wife was killed and from then on had stopped caring about the future.

'Sorry,' Lorna said, seeing his pained expression. 'I didn't mean to hit a nerve.'

'I thought we'd quit bee-sweetening each another?'

'What do you mean?'

'You'd drown a kitten if it benefitted you.'

'Ouch,' Lorna said. 'I really *did* hit a nerve, didn't I?'

'Don't flatter yourself. My skin's thicker than that.'

'Then tell me why a man like you drifts.'

'It suits me. I like the solitude. I like being in different places. And most of all, I like not having to answer to anyone or deal with problems I didn't cause myself.'

'I envy you for that.'

'Why? What problems could you have? You just said you were making money hand over fist.'

'Money's not my problem. You are.'

'Me? How?'

'Curtis and I were counting on Joe to ramrod this enterprise we've been planning.'

'Curtis being the fella in your bed?'

'One of the brothel beds, not mine,' Lorna corrected. 'There's a difference.'

'Fair enough. And without Joe Holly, you're a man short? That the problem?'

'Yes — unless, of course, you'd be interested in taking his place?'

'That'd depend on the enterprise.'

'I can't reveal that yet.'

'Then my answer's no. I don't sign on blind — not even for a beautiful woman.'

'That's too bad. I want you in on this.'

'Then sweeten the pot.'

'I can't. Not yet. But if you'll trust me for a few days, Curtis and I will then show our cards to everyone involved.'

'Then ask me again in a few days . . .'

'Wait!' Lorna said as Coop finished dressing and stood up. 'Why're you going?'

'I figured we were all talked out.'

Lorna sighed, knowing she was cornered. 'All right, you win. I can't tell you what we're planning, but I can say that Holly's share was five thousand — in gold!'

Coop whistled softly as he buckled on his gunbelt.

'Does that mean you're interested?'

'Enough to ask a final question: This fella Curtis, does he have a first name?'

'Yes. But he hates it.'

'Then you better tell me what it is, so I don't happen to call him by it.'

'Gospel.'

'*Gospel?*'

'I know, I know, it's hard to believe anyone would name their child Gospel. But Curtis' folks were Southern Baptists and saw no fault in it. Unfortunately not everyone was as understanding. They made Curtis' life hell till he found a way to stop them.'

'With lead?'

'Exactly. No one teases a fast gun, as well you know.'

'Because I'm also a gunfighter?'

'With a reputation that far exceeds Curtis'. So to use your words: quit acting modest. It doesn't suit you.'

Coop winced. 'Ouch, as a lady I know once said.'

Lorna laughed. 'Anyway, you can't leave because I want you to meet Curtis.'

'Later. First I got to stable and grain the horses.'

'But you *will* be back — afterward, I mean?'

'Five thousand in gold is tough to walk away from.'

'Yet you're thinking of doing exactly

that, aren't you?'

Coop shrugged noncommittally.

'How can I change your mind?'

'Knowing when I'll get paid might help.'

'As soon as our little enterprise pays off.'

Coop considered the offer, then said: 'Throw in Holly's horse and you got a deal.'

'Done!' Lorna offered him her hand.

Coop shook it, tipped his hat, '*Adios*,' and left.

Lorna donned her robe, went to the front door, opened it and waved her hand.

Immediately Foley, Crouch and Wallace approached from a nearby alley.

'Don't let that man out of your sight,' Lorna told Foley.

'What if he tries to leave town?'

'Stop him.'

'And if he don't want to be stopped?'

'Dammit, use your imagination!' She slammed the door in his face.

6

Henson's livery stable was next to the telegraph office at the end of the main street. One of the town's first buildings, its adobe walls had been scarred by years of desert winds and needed whitewashing. But the interior was clean and there was fresh hay in the loft and Coop gladly led the horses inside. As he did, he glanced back and smiled grimly as he saw Foley, Crouch and Wallace watching him from a nearby alley.

As he paused by the first stall, he was confronted by a freckled, dimple-cheeked, red-haired youth in a patched check-ered shirt and ragged jeans.

'Help you, mister?'

'Stall and grain 'em, boy.'

'I ain't no boy,' the youth said defiantly.

Coop peered closer and realized he

was looking at a barefoot girl in her early teens. Her face, though pretty, was smudged with dirt and her boyishly short hair looked as if it had been cut with blunt garden shears. But Coop, like everyone else, didn't notice her shortcomings — he was too captured by her large agate-green eyes.

'I reckon you ain't at that,' he admitted. 'But it's not for lack of trying.'

'What's that supposed to mean?'

'Well, you got to admit, missy, you ain't done much with what God give you.'

'Costs money to look beautiful,' the girl said. 'So unless you're figuring on paying for me to get fixed up . . . ' She left the rest unsaid and coyly fluttered her lashes.

'I'll think on it,' Coop said, amused by her flirting.

'Well, while you're thinking, how long you figuring on boarding this crow bait?'

'Two . . . maybe three days at most.'

The girl eyed the roan suspiciously. 'So these horses, they're both yourn?'

'What makes you think they ain't?'

'Nothing,' she lied. 'Just asking in case somebody else claims the roan is his.'

'That ain't likely to happen, missy. Now, how much do I owe you?'

'Two bits, mister.'

'Fair enough.' Coop dug out a quarter and dropped it in her outstretched hand.

'For each horse,' she added impudently.

'Any *other* hidden charges?'

'Nope. That's it.'

Coop gave her another quarter, then grabbed his carbine and saddlebags and left.

The girl turned to the rear stall. 'How'd I do, gramps?'

An old man with watery, red-rimmed blue eyes, a gray stubble and a halo of white curls shuffled out holding a .12-gauge shotgun.

'You done fine, Myla — 'cept for your flirting.'

'I wasn't flirting,' Myla Lufton said

indignantly. 'I was just being sociable.'

'Call it what you like,' her grand-father said. 'Just cut it out.'

Myla scowled, and to get back at him, said: 'You *do* know whose red roan this is, don't you, gramps?'

Her grandfather gave the horse another look. 'Jumping Judas!' he exclaimed as he suddenly recognized the red roan. 'Why the deuce didn't you say something before?'

'I figured you'd recognize it, too.'

'I would've, if I knew where my darn specs were.'

'Where they always are,' Myla taunted. ' — on top of your head.'

Grumbling, her grandfather pulled the wire-framed spectacles down onto his nose.

'So what do you think, gramps? You reckon we should tell the sheriff?'

'Tell him what? That this gunfighter showed up with Joe Holly's horse?'

'A horse that Joe would never, *ever* sell,' Myla reminded. 'Not for no reason!'

'That ain't none of our business. Not

if we want to stay healthy.'

'But that's my point. Sooner or later Joe Holly's going to find out we got his horse stalled here and right off, he's going to be mighty sore that we never told him. Of course, you know best, gramps.' Myla added, her tone suggesting otherwise. 'I mean, like you're always saying, I'm nothing but a scatterbrained filly barely past teething.' She led the horses to the stalls, pleased that she'd gotten in the last word.

7

Coop entered the Holy Moses, paused just inside the door and looked around for Lorna. He saw she was behind the bar, collecting money from the cash register. The shorter of the two bartenders, who'd seen Coop enter, spoke to her. She immediately closed the cash-drawer, ducked under the end of the bar and started upstairs. Halfway up, she looked back and nodded for Coop to follow her. She then continued on up to the gallery. There, she waited until he joined her and then led him back to her office.

'I want you to meet Curtis,' Lorna said. 'But first a word of caution: Curtis looks harmless, but don't be fooled by his girlish looks or long golden curls. He's got an ugly mean streak and no conscience. And if that isn't enough, he suffers from these awful pains in his belly, which doesn't improve his disposition. So, don't prod him, okay, because he'll have no qualms shooting you.'

'Sounds like the ideal personality for a bank robber,' Coop said.

Lorna gave him a sour look. 'Save your sarcasm, Mr. Cooper. This isn't the time for it.' Opening the door, she led him inside.

The office was small and comfortably furnished. It also smelled of New Orleans' perfume mingled with cheap Mexican cigars. Coop saw that the pungent odor came from a green cheroot being smoked by a tall lean man sitting behind a polished mahogany desk. In his mid-twenties, he was clean shaven, wore a tailored western suit and the boots propped up on the desk were custom made. Effeminately handsome, he had shoulder-length curly blond hair, perfect features and pale blue eyes that he'd inherited from his Scandinavian mother.

Coop had never met a man who was beautiful, but he couldn't help thinking that Curtis fitted the bill. Presently, though, the gunman was trying to relieve his boredom by flicking playing cards into a wastebasket. He looked up and tensed as he saw Coop. His left hand inched toward a fancy nickel-plated Colt .38, double-action Lightning revolver with ivory grips tucked in a shoulder holster under his velvet-lapelled jacket.

'Curtis,' Lorna said, hoping to stop any trouble. 'I'd like you to meet Morgan — '

' — Cooper,' finished Gospel Curtis.

'Do you know me, mister?' Coop said, trying to place the blond gunman.

'Heard of you.'

'Oh.'

'Heard of me?'

'Can't say as I have,' Coop said.

His tone was dismissive and Gospel resented it. His lips tightened about the cheroot and his eyes narrowed menacingly. 'Then you can't be from around here.'

'That sounds almost like a threat.'

'Take it any way you like,' Gospel said. 'Makes no matter to me.'

Coop drew, so swiftly his gun seemed

to jump into his hand, and aimed at Gospel's foot. 'How about I shoot off one of your toes, sonny? Reckon that might *matter* to you?'

Gospel, impressed by Coop's fast draw but at the same time not wanting to lose a toe, quickly removed his boots from the desktop and sat upright in the chair.

'Was that a yes or a no?' Coop asked, so innocently Lorna had to laugh.

'I don't think Curtis knows,' she said. She walked around the desk and stood in front of Gospel. 'For the first time in his life he's jolly well — flummoxed!'

Gospel glowered at Lorna, then at Coop. 'You got the drop on me this time, mister, ain't no denying that. But it won't ever happen again. Count on it!'

'Really?' Coop holstered his six-shooter. 'Care to prove that?'

'Some other time,' Gospel said. ' — when Miss Lorna ain't around.'

'If that's all that's troubling you, let's go outside and settle this right now — sonny!'

'Stop it, both of you!' Lorna snapped.

'I need guns, *live* guns, not dead hot-heads!'

For another tense moment the gunfighters glared at each other.

Then Coop grinned. 'Don't take it personal, sonny. Just because I ain't heard of you don't mean squat. Hell, I'd never heard of Billy the Kid till Pat Garrett introduced us.'

'You know Sheriff Garrett?' Gospel said, impressed.

'Doesn't every gunfighter worth his salt?'

Knowing he was being baited, Gospel's hand inched closer to his holstered gun.

Fearing gunplay, Lorna said: 'Curtis, would you mind getting out of my chair?'

He minded but obeyed her anyway, languidly uncoiling his long thin body until he was on his feet. He was taller than Coop but didn't look it due to his slumped posture.

'Ain't she a dilly?' he said derisively.

Lorna spoke before Coop could. 'He

doesn't know me well enough to know *what* I am, Curtis. But he will in time, because he's agreed to join our little enterprise.'

'So I've heard,' Gospel began — then broke off, grunting as pain knifed through his abdomen. It only last a few seconds, but it hurt enough to make him sweat. 'But only after you gave him Joe Holly's horse, right?'

'How'd you know that, Curtis?'

'I got my ear to the ground, Miss Lorna.'

'Well, I figured it was a small price to pay. Now,' she added, 'if you don't mind, I have work to do. So if you two gentlemen will excuse me, I'll get started on it.'

Coop wasn't offended by her dismissive tone, but Gospel reacted as if he'd been slapped. Trying to salvage what little remained of his pride, he turned to Coop, saying: 'I could use a drink. Join me?'

'Sure,' Coop said.

'Good idea,' Lorna said as the two

gunmen turned to leave. 'It'll give you both a chance to get to know each other. Oh, and Curtis, while you're at it, be sure to tell the bartender that the drinks are on me.'

8

The bar was still crowded but the taller of the two bartenders, on seeing Gospel approaching with Coop told the men drinking in front of him to move, making room for the two gunmen.

'Dos tequilas — on the house,' Gospel ordered. 'And leave the bottle!'

'Yes, sir.' The tall bartender quickly poured the drinks and walked away.

'Free booze?' Coop remarked. 'Now that's something I could get used to.'

'Why pay when you can get it free, I always say.'

'Amen.' Coop grinned and raised his glass in a toast. 'Here's to good luck, sonny, and plenty of gold in our saddle-bags!'

'Don't call me sonny!' Gospel snapped. 'I ain't partial to it.'

'Fair enough.'

'As for good luck, we don't need any.

We got the bank manager in our pocket.'

'We?' queried Coop.

'Me and the boss.'

'You mean, Miss Lorna?'

'Nah. She ain't the boss. She just likes to pretend she is.'

'Then who're we talking about?'

'You'll know when you meet him.'

'When's that going to be?'

'After we rob the bank.'

'And this 'boss' — you sure we can trust him?'

'To the hilt. Hell, he's the one who bribed the bank manager. Without him, there wouldn't be no robbery. 'Least, not one that's foolproof.'

'Good,' Coop said. 'I been in prison and I didn't like it.'

'Stick with me,' Gospel promised. 'You'll never have to worry about prison again. Your only problem will be finding saddlebags big enough to hold all your gold!'

'I'll drink to that.'

They finished their tequilas and

Gospel poured two more. As they drank, he studied Coop as if trying to figure him out.

'If you got something on your mind,' Coop said, 'speak your piece.'

'Okay,' Curtis said. 'It's Lorna.'

'What about her?'

'She's important to me.'

'Meaning, she's your woman?'

'Not like you're suggesting, no.'

Coop frowned. 'You're going to have to stretch that out for me.'

'Maybe later. When I get to know you better.'

'Fair enough. But let me say this: if your job is to protect her from strangers or the local yahoos, rest assured, you don't have to raise a sweat over me.'

'That's good to know.'

'Don't get me wrong. Miss Lorna, she's prettier than a desert sunset. But she recruited me, not the other way 'round. I mean, but for her I'd be in Mexico right now, headed for the nearest whorehouse.'

Gospel weighed Coop's words and decided he was telling the truth. 'I'm glad to hear that. Miss Lorna, she's been hurt enough and I aim to see it don't happen again. Besides, *amigo*, I've taken a hankering to you and that don't happen too often.'

'To me, either. Let's shake on it.'

They shook hands. There was a sudden murmuring in the saloon. Coop and Gospel looked up at the gallery just as Lorna emerged from her office. She smiled and waved to the customers, bringing whoops and cheers from them.

Enjoying the limelight, she made her way to the stairs, her long gold lame gown shimmering in the lights almost as brightly as her twinkling diamonds.

'You're wrong about that sunset,' Gospel told Coop.

'How?'

'Lorna's prettier than the sun, the moon and all the stars put together.'

'Can't dispute that,' admitted Coop. 'Any fella who has her on his arm has got to feel like he's holding four aces.'

'Yeah,' agreed Gospel. 'That sums her up perfectly!'

9

The next morning Coop and Gospel, wearing long tan dusters and wide-brimmed hats pulled low over their faces, rode up to the bank. There, they dismounted and took their time tying their horses to the rail. Shortly, they were joined by Foley and then the two gunmen, Crouch and Wallace, all similarly dressed.

Greeting each other with curt nods, they glanced around to make sure the townspeople weren't watching them. Then, satisfied that no one suspected anything, they pulled their bandanas over their faces and entered the bank.

Inside, several customers were lined up at the tellers' cages. Their backs were to the door and none of them noticed the five masked men enter. Neither did the tellers nor the fat, gray-haired manager, Wendell Blackburn, seated at his desk behind the cages.

The five men moved quickly. Gospel locked the door, pulled the shades down and told Crouch and Wallace to stand guard. Then, guns drawn, he, Coop and Foley told the now-alarmed customers to get down on the floor. They obeyed quickly. So did the tellers when Coop ordered them to open their cash-drawers. As for the bank manager, he protested just long enough to hide the fact that he was involved and then obeyed Gospel's orders and opened the vault.

Once the big steel door was open, Foley kept everyone covered while Coop and Gospel entered the vault. There, they quickly filled gunny sacks with pokes of miners' gold dust, trays of silver dollars, a dozen gold bars and stacks of greenbacks. But not wanting to overload their horses should they be pursued, they ignored the boxes of loose change and hurried out.

'Any of you tries to follow us,' Gospel warned everyone, 'you'll be gunned down. Is that clear?'

They all nodded fearfully.

'C'mon!' Wallace yelled. 'Folks outside are wondering why the bank's closed!'

'Quit panicking,' Gospel growled, 'and open the goddamn door!'

Wallace unlocked the door and the five gunmen hurried out to their horses. Quickly untying them, they mounted and rode off. The few townspeople gathered outside made no attempt to stop them. They just stood there, as if mesmerized, and watched as the robbers galloped away . . . leaving nothing behind but their departing dust.

10

Once out of town Coop, Gospel and the other gunmen lowered their bandanas and rode across the border into Mexico. There, safe from pursuit, they reined up under some trees and rested their horses.

'What'd I tell you fellas?' Gospel grinned. 'Easy as robbing the blind!'

'Maybe easier,' Coop said. 'So, where we headed now, *compadre*?'

Gospel pointed at a dry riverbed that crossed the trail ahead and fed into a steep-walled canyon. 'We follow this arroyo till we come to a gully. There's a stream nearby and some ruins. We'll water the horses there and split up the money.'

'Fair enough,' Coop said. 'Let's ride!'

'Hold it!' Foley snarled.

'What's your problem?' Gospel demanded.

Foley thumbed at Coop. 'Him.'

'Meaning?'

'Is he giving the orders now?'

Gospel scowled at the rat-faced little gunman. 'He is if I want him to and right now I want him to. Got it?' As he spoke, Gospel's left hand moved to his holstered Colt.

'Sure,' Foley said sourly: 'I just wanted to know who's running things, that's all.'

'Well, 'know' this,' Gospel warned. 'No matter who it is, it ain't you! So keep your damn' mouth shut and start riding, like Coop said!'

Foley seethed, but as usual fear controlled his rage and he spurred his horse away.

Gospel glared after him. 'Goddamned little weasel. I should've pistol-whipped some manners into him years ago.'

On reaching the gully, Gospel led Coop and the others to an old adobe ruins that was built up against the cliffs. A stream curved past the ruins. Dismounting beside it, they loosened the saddle cinches and let their weary horses drink. They then carried the gunnysacks into the crumbling buildings and began emptying them. They dumped out all the money but not the gold bars, which Gospel insisted remain in the sacks.

Foley knew better than to question Gospel, but Crouch and Wallace demanded to know what the hell was going on.

'You said we were all getting equal shares,' Wallace grumbled.

'We are,' Gospel said. ''Cept for the gold. That ain't included.'

'In other words, you're hogging it all for yourself?'

'Wrong. I ain't getting none of it!'

'Then who the hell is?'

'The boss, who else?'

'Miss Lorna, you mean?'

'Hell, no,' said Gospel. 'The real boss — ' He broke off as Crouch jammed a gun into his ribs.

'Either we get our share of that gold, Curtis, or you get a dose of lead.'

'Reckon I got no choice,' Gospel said. He paused, wincing as a sudden pain shot through his lower abdomen, and then thumbed at the gunnysacks containing the gold bars. 'So, go ahead. Help yourselves.'

'That's better,' Crouch said. Then to Wallace: 'Count out our shares, partner.'

Wallace nodded and began untying one of the gunnysacks.

'You might as well take it all,' Gospel said. 'Because either way, you're dead.'

'Why?' said Wallace. 'All we're taking is our share. That's only fair, ain't it?'

'Fair's got nothing to do with it,' said Gospel. 'The deal was if the boss bribed the bank manager then the gold was his. Those were his terms and he's going to be mighty pissed if we don't stick to 'em.'

'Too bad,' Crouch said. 'I ain't sharing my cut with no one!'

'Me neither,' Wallace said, adding: 'You should've told us about this before the robbery, Curtis. That way, Ned and me could've decided if we wanted to throw in with you — ' He got no further as Foley slid a derringer from his sleeve and shot him.

Shocked, Crouch whirled around to shoot Foley.

Before he could, Gospel jerked his Colt and shot him.

Coop, worried he might be next, drew his revolver and faced Gospel and Foley.

'Unless you want to join those two,' he said, thumbing at the dead gunmen, 'drop your guns. Do it,' he added as Foley hesitated. 'Or I might remember what a pleasure it would be to put a hole in your miserable hide!'

Grudgingly, Foley obeyed. 'I won't forget this,' he snarled. 'My day will come.'

'From what I hear,' Gospel said, 'your day's already come — *and* gone.'

'How do you mean?'

'In the saloon, when you and Coop first met. He gave you a chance to jerk your iron and you faded.'

'That weren't my doing,' Foley grumbled. 'Miss Lorna was calling the shots.'

'Lucky for you she was,' Coop said. 'Otherwise, you wouldn't be standing here.'

Enraged, Foley started to pick up his gun and then stopped.

'What's wrong?' Coop taunted. 'Having trouble with your yellow streak again?'

'I ain't no fool,' Foley raged. 'If I try to pick up my iron, you'll shoot me.'

Coop laughed mirthlessly. 'If that's all that's stopping you, let me help you.' He picked up Foley's gun, stuffed it in his holster and stepped back. 'Any more excuses?'

Foley licked his lips, desperate to draw but lacking the nerve.

'Jesus!' Gospel exclaimed. 'Slap leather, you gutless little turd.'

Foley flinched as if punched but still couldn't find the guts to draw.

Gospel spat disgustedly at Foley's feet, then said to Coop: 'C'mon. We're wasting time here. If I don't get this gold to the boss, he'll think I've double-crossed him and send his vultures after me.'

'Go ahead, pick up your iron,' Coop said. 'Not you,' he added as Foley bent down to pick up his gun. 'Like you once told me: I got bigger plans for you.'

Foley straightened up, eyes burning with hatred. 'You don't scare me none, mister. A lot can happen between here and Rocas Rojas.'

'You're so right,' Gospel said. He reached back as if to grab the hat hanging behind his neck. But at the last instant, he slipped his hand under his shirt, pulled a knife from a sheath and with a flick of his wrist, threw it at Foley.

It buried in the little gunman's heart. He staggered back and collapsed. Dead.

Gospel pulled the knife from Foley's chest, wiped the blade on the gunman's shirt and grinned at Coop. 'Now you don't have to worry none about trusting the bastard.'

'True,' Coop said, adding: 'You're a

man of many surprises, Mr. Curtis.'

Gospel chuckled callously. 'That's what makes me interesting, don't you know?' Picking up one of the gunnysacks containing six of the gold bars, he hefted it over his shoulder and walked out of the ruins.

Coop eyed the three corpses on the floor. 'Rot in hell,' he muttered. Then picking up the other gunnysack, he hurried out after Gospel.

11

The two of them rode parallel to the border for several hours before finally reining up in front of an old adobe archway on which was carved: *Cielo Vista Rancho*.

Dismounting to give their weary horses a breather, Coop and Gospel sat on a rock and rolled a smoke. As they lit up, Coop looked around. There were no fences or signs warning trespassers not to ride across the parched, sundrenched desert that stretched to the far-off hills, yet he sensed they were being watched.

'Whose land is this?' he asked Gospel.

'Don Del Gardo's.'

'Is he the 'boss' you mentioned — the one who's getting the gold?'

'Yeah. I figured it was time you two met — Argh!' Gospel doubled over in agony.

'You ought to see a doc' about those

pains,' Coop said. 'Could be serious.'

Gospel shrugged it off. 'Nah. They only last for a few seconds and then they always go away — ' He stopped as a group of armed *vaqueros* in black-and-silver uniforms and matching sombreros suddenly rode out from behind some rocks and surrounded them. All were mounted on magnificent black stallions with flowing manes and tails and their high-pommeled Mexican saddles were decorated with silver *conchos*.

'Keep your hand away from your iron,' Gospel warned Coop. 'They're just here to escort us to the *hacienda*.'

'Some welcoming committee!'

'They're harmless. Just play along with them. You'll find it worthwhile.' He turned to the leader, a short, big-bellied Mexican in a fancy dark-blue uniform flamboyantly decorated with gold braid and Colonel's insignias. About forty, Colonel Abelardo had fierce dark eyes, a large nose that hooked down over a thin, waxed mustache, and an arrogant sneering face that was shaded from the sun by the peak of a gold-braided cap.

'*Buenas tardes, coronel*,' Gospel said, smiling. 'All goes well, I hope?'

'*Si, Senor* Curtis. It goes most well.' Col. Abelardo paused and stared disparagingly at Coop. 'But I am compelled to ask why you bring this *gringo* here? You know Don Del Gardo's rules. No *Yanquis*!'

'Without this *Yanqui*,' Gospel replied, '*El Jefe* would be short six bars of gold! But of course, *coronel*,' he taunted, 'if you want to ignore your orders, I'll tell my friend he ain't welcome and he'll happily return the gold to the bank in Rocas Rojas!'

Stung, Abelardo hid his anger behind a contemptuous smile and stroked his neatly trimmed mustache. He made no attempt to hide his dislike for Gospel and Coop guessed the Colonel only tolerated the gunman because of his relationship with Don Del Gardo. But Coop could tell it stuck in the Colonel's craw and he wasn't surprised when the officer said sarcastically: 'It is most kind of you to remind me of this, *Senor* Curtis. You are right. A soldier must always obey orders! So, if you *gringos* will follow me, I'll take you to *El Jefe!*' He whirled his stallion around and barked orders to the *vaqueros*. They obediently formed two columns, one on either side of Coop and Gospel, ready to escort them to the *hacienda*.

Col. Abelardo brandished his saber, '*Vamos!*' and spurred his stallion forward.

Coop and Gospel and the *vaqueros* rode after him.

'Seems to me,' Coop said to Gospel, 'this Abelardo *hombre* don't cotton to you.'

'You picked up on that, did you?' said Gospel, laughing. 'Now why do you think that is, *amigo*? I mean, just because you steal a fella's wife and hump the daylights out of her don't mean he should take it personal — especially since the sonofabitch treated her worse than a skinned polecat.'

'Just goes to show you,' Coop

deadpanned. 'When it comes to the ladies, some men are just naturally narrow-minded.'

'Ain't that the truth?' Gospel said. 'Now me, I favor a little variety — ' He winced as pain knotted his belly and then said: 'While we're on the subject of ladies, Del Gardo's got three daughters who're prettier than a creek full of trout.'

'Thanks. I'll be sure to keep my jeans buttoned up.'

'Around them, that ain't always easy.'

'Meaning?'

'Well, though *El Jefe* acts like they're all virgins, behind his back they're ready to jump into bed with almost any *gringo* they meet.'

'Just what I need,' Coop grumbled. 'Some *loco* father chasing me with a goddamn machete! Judas priest, do you reckon it's too late to ride back across the border?'

'Depends on how much you value your life.'

'Meaning the Colonel wouldn't appreciate it?'

'That's putting it mildly,' Gospel said. 'Hell, we so much as fart the wrong way and the sonofabitch will use it as an excuse to have his men shoot off our *cajones*!'

12

Led by Col. Abelardo, the *vaqueros* escorted Coop and Gospel across the barren desert, on into a narrow gorge framed by towering rock walls that echoed with the pounding of their horses' hooves.

It was stifling hot in the gorge and Coop was grateful when they finally left it and entered Carbon Canyon. A dry riverbed snaked between the canyon's black cliffs while high overhead, circling hawks drifted on the thermals as they searched for prey.

Finally, after a mile or so, the canyon fed into a green valley that Gospel called: '*Jardin del Eden*.' Low brown hills walled in the valley like silent guardians. And as Coop and the others rode between them he was surprised by the abrupt change in flora. The valley was full of wild flowers, feathery-tipped pampas grass and flowering cacti, their brilliant colors brightening the grassland on which grazed a herd of cattle.

Though Coop was familiar with the land on both sides of the border, the valley was new to him and as he looked around he couldn't help thinking that Gospel was right: this was Mexico's answer to the Garden of Eden.

They rode at a steady lope until they reached the far end of the valley. Here, they reined up before large wrought-iron gates that guarded the entrance to an imposing *hacienda* surrounded by high adobe walls. One of the *vaqueros* dismounted and opened the gates, allowing Coop, Gospel and the others to enter a paved circular courtyard adorned with brilliant red, white and purple bougainvillea.

'Whoever this Del Gardo is,' Coop said as they dismounted and tied up their horses, 'he sure knows how to live high on the hog.'

'If I'd inherited this spread and all his money,' Gospel grumbled, 'so would I.'

'If he's already rich, why the hell's he

risking everything by rustling beef?'

Gospel gave a scoffing laugh. 'First off, he ain't risking nothing. This is Mexico, *amigo*. Rich or poor, everyone steals. It's a way of life down here. In fact, folks think you're stupid if you *don't* steal.'

'What about the *Federales* or the *Rurales*, don't they have a say in this?'

'You serious? Those sonsofbitches are the worst thieves of all. They'd steal from a blind cripple! Not that I blame them. Hell, why should they care? They're the law. They see something they like, they take it. Don't matter if it's a ranch, livestock or some fella's wife — it's theirs! And you better not argue, else they'll gun you down!'

'*Silencio, senores!*' Col. Abelardo said fiercely. 'Come! Follow me!'

'Charming sonofabitch, ain't he?' Coop muttered as he and Gospel accompanied the Colonel to the massive, hand-carved front door.

'He's also the cruelest bastard you'll ever meet,' Gospel said. ' — especially when it comes to torture. Judas, he's invented ways to cause pain that defy the imagination.'

'If he's everything you say he is, how come you ain't put a bullet in him?'

'I've thought about it, but then I figured what'd be the point? The fella who takes his place wouldn't be no better. Hell, he might even be worse!'

They entered the cool, sprawling house and followed Col. Abelardo across a large red-tiled foyer framed by tall, sunlit windows that led to a shaded patio.

There, a small, middle-aged, elegantly-dressed man sat in a big hand-carved chair admiring the flowers that grew abundantly in a spacious, walled garden. His back was to Coop and Gospel and it wasn't until after he dismissed the Colonel and turned to greet them that they saw his face.

Coop gaped as he realized he was looking at the shabby, insignificant little piano player in the Holy Moses — except, the now-clean-shaven man was no longer shabby or insignificant-looking. Instead he looked resplendent in a tailored black outfit and black boots and exuded a confident, authoritative personality that was compelling.

Amused by Coop's shocked reaction, the man rose and bowed politely, saying: 'I am Don Edwin Del Gardo. It is a pleasure to finally meet you, *Senor* Cooper.'

Momentarily lost for words, Coop could only shake his head. 'Forgive my bad manners, *senor*,' he said finally. 'But you truly had me fooled.'

'For this deception, I beg your forgiveness,' Del Gardo apologized. 'But in this world, we all lead many lives. Do we not?'

'I reckon so,' Coop agreed, looking about him. 'Some better than others.'

'This is true, *senor*. But putting my wealth aside, now that you are aware of my plans, I'm sure you agree that secrecy is most necessary if I am to continue to — to — ' Unable to find the right phrase, Del Gardo turned to Gospel, asking: 'What is that amusing expression you use to describe eavesdropping?'

'Keeping my ear to the ground?'

'Exactly,' Del Gardo said. Then to Coop: ' — to keep my ear to the ground without arousing undue suspicion?'

'I do agree, *senor*. And I assure you, I'm grateful to be included in your plans.'

'From what Colonel Abelardo tells me, I am the one who should be grateful. A prize such as this,' Del Gardo continued, indicating the two sacks holding the gold bars, 'is enough to tempt even the most honest of men.'

Coop shrugged. 'Like they say, *senor* — honor among thieves.'

'Ah, yes,' Del Gardo said. 'So it is spoken, so it must be.' Turning to Gospel, he added: 'After we have broken bread, there is much to discuss.'

'You mean another robbery? It's okay,' Gospel said when Del Gardo hesitated and gave Coop a guarded look. 'You can talk in front of him. He's one of us now.'

'You misunderstand, *mi amigo*,' Del Gardo replied. 'My caution has nothing to do with my trust of *Senor* Cooper or anyone else within these walls. It is merely that I feel it would be more civilized if we dined together before discussing business.'

'I'm all for that,' Gospel grinned. 'Been so long since I ate a sit-down meal, I can't remember what real food tastes like.'

13

The three of them sat at a massive, hand-carved table on the terrace overlooking the rear wall of the property and, beyond, a grassy plain that stretched to the distant hills.

There was a fourth place set across the table from Coop and he wondered who would be joining them. He hadn't long to wait. Once the white-jacketed manservant had served them wine in silver goblets, a tall slender girl entered. About seventeen, she had her father's black hair, cut so that it hung loosely about her shoulders and was pretty in a shy, withdrawn way that Coop found appealing. She also faintly reminded him of Helen, though he couldn't think why and quickly dismissed it.

The girl paused beside Del Gardo and gave him a perfunctory kiss on the cheek before sitting at the table. Then making sure her father wasn't looking, she smiled at Gospel in a way that hinted there were secrets between them. Gospel smiled back in the same fashion, something Coop stored away. The girl then shyly lowered her dark exquisite eyes as her father proudly introduced her to Coop as his daughter, Gabriela.

She did not speak or look up during introductions and Coop sensed she'd rather be anywhere but there. At the same time he wondered why she and her father were at odds. But intrigued by her, he watched as she sat there, nervously twisting the ends of her long hair around one finger.

'*Para!*' Del Gardo said sharply. 'You know how that irritates me, child!'

Gabriela stopped twisting her hair and said angrily: 'I am not a child, papa! I am a grown woman and I wish you'd treat me as such, especially in front of strangers.'

Her outburst surprised Coop. She obviously wasn't as shy as she looked. Even so, he wondered how she dared scold her father so disrespectfully in front of company, and waited to see how Del Gardo would respond.

The angry Don never got the chance as Gospel quickly intervened.

'Tell me, Gabby,' he said to Gabriela, 'where're your beautiful step-sisters today?'

'Gone,' she replied sadly.

'Gone?' Gospel looked puzzled. 'Gone where?'

'Ask papa,' she said sullenly.

'I enrolled Isabel and Sophia at St. Magdalena's,' Del Gardo said before Gospel could question him.

'Mean that big convent in Mexico City?'

'*Si.*'

'For the sake of wild horses, why?'

'Personal reasons, Curtis.'

Before Gospel could respond, Gabriela said: 'Do not waste your breath. Surely you know by now that papa never discusses family matters with outsiders.'

'*Muérdele la lengue!*' her father snapped.

'No, Gabby's right,' Gospel said. 'I've

heard you say that many times. It's just — well, I figured by now I *was* family. 'Least, that's what you've told me often enough.'

Embarrassed, the fiery Don softened. 'Forgive me, *mi amigo*. In no way did I mean to make you to feel otherwise.'

Gospel shrugged. 'Ah, forget it, Edwin. It ain't worth fussing over. I just wondered where Sophia and Isabel were, that's all. I care about them and — '

'I too care about them,' said Del Gardo. 'They are my daughters and I love them deeply. But I could no longer deal with their defiant behavior — ' He stopped, realizing that by demeaning his daughters he was also demeaning the family name, and then said quickly: 'Believe me, it was not an easy decision. In fact, as a father and a still-grieving widower, it was the most difficult one I've ever made.'

'Then, why'd you make it?' Gospel asked. 'Isabel and Sophia ain't mean-spirited. They're just a pair of fun-loving fillies, kicking up their heels and sniffing the wind.' Even as he spoke, he saw Del Gardo flush and knew he had insulted him, something he'd had no intention of doing. 'Please forgive me, old friend,' he apologized. 'I didn't mean to butt into your family's affairs. I respect you too much to ever do that. It's just, I'm mighty fond of your daughters and realizing I wasn't going to see them, kind of kicked the dust out of me and I spoke without using my brains.'

It was the longest speech Coop had ever heard Gospel make and he realized his friend was more deeply involved with Del Gardo's step-daughters than he'd let on.

'There is no need for you to apologize,' Del Gardo assured. 'And I understand your disappointment. I, too, am disappointed — in my daughters and myself. Nevertheless, it was a decision that had to be made for their own good.'

'*Your* good, you mean,' Gabriela said.

'*Silencio!*'

Gabriela hesitated, reluctant to defy her father. But unable to control her anger, she said to Gospel and Coop: 'I speak the truth. My sisters were so desperate to be free of father's suffocating discipline they accepted offers of marriage from men many times their age — men they did not love. But even this humiliation did not permit them to escape from this — *prison!*'

'Wait a minute,' Gospel said, alarmed. 'Are you saying they're hitched?'

'No,' Gabriela replied. 'When the men asked my father for his permission to marry my sisters, he refused to give it. Instead, he punished my sisters by sending them to St. Magdalena's.'

'Nonsense!' Del Gardo protested weakly. 'That was not the reason.' He turned to Coop, hoping to appeal to the only person who wasn't against him. 'The truth is, *senor*, much as I love my daughters, trying to control their rebellious nature finally became too much for me. No matter how well I treated them, they insisted on acting like adolescents, instead of ladies, as their beloved mother desired. I put up with them until finally their disobedience became such a distraction it interfered with my duties as a rancher and, more importantly, *patron* to the villagers.'

'So he shipped them off,' Gabriela said bitterly, 'just like cattle!'

'Gabriela,' her father exclaimed, 'how dare you insult me in front of our guests!'

Gabriela, realizing she'd gone too far, toned down her defiance. 'I'm sorry, papa. I didn't mean to insult you or dishonor the family name, but in your heart you know what I say is true.'

'I know no such thing!'

'Then why did I overhear you tell Father Crespi that you only sent Isabel and Sophia away because they were threatening to elope, just to defy you?'

Stung by the truth, Del Gardo swallowed before saying: 'Be quiet, daughter! You have disgraced me enough. We will speak no more of this matter. Is that understood?'

Gabriela started to respond, realized it was useless, and got to her feet.

'Sit down!' her father ordered. 'I did not give you permission to leave the table.'

Gabriela stood there for a moment, glaring at him. Then she nodded politely to Coop and Gospel, '*Perdone, senores*,' and defiantly walked away.

Del Gardo reddened, almost apoplectic with rage, but said nothing.

Gabriela crossed the terrace and on reaching the arched doorway leading indoors, paused and glared at her father. 'You're always telling me how much you love me, papa, but do not think I'm not aware of your plans.'

'Plans?' Del Gardo said, pretending to be puzzled. 'What plans are you talking about?'

'The ones involving my future,' Gabriela said. Then as he started to protest: 'Oh, you can deny it all you want, papa. It doesn't matter. Nothing can alter the fact that if I had not been visiting Aunt Theresa when you sent my sisters away, you would have sent me with them!'

Before Del Gardo could reply, Gabriela stormed into the house.

In her hurry, she almost bumped into a servant who was wheeling in a small cart containing a silver cauldron of cold corn chowder and silver soup bowls. But at the last instant she avoided him and hurried to her room.

'Please excuse my daughter's poor manners,' Del Gardo said to Coop. 'Her dear mother died when Gabriela was still an infant, and ever since she has been angry at the world and everyone in it.'

'I'm sorry to hear that,' Coop said. 'But I understand her anger. For a long time after my wife was killed, I felt the same way.'

'Your wife was killed?' Del Gardo said, dismayed.

'Yes. Raped and then shot by three outlaws who stopped at our ranch for water.'

'*Madre de Dios!*' exclaimed Del

Gardo. 'What kind of world do we live in that repays kindness with such degenerate acts?'

'It don't end there, neither,' said Gospel. 'The bastards weren't satisfied with killing his wife — they slaughtered his livestock and burned his house down as well!'

'But these outlaws,' Del Gardo said, 'why would they do such a despicable thing?'

'If you're asking if I had any prior trouble with them,' Coop said, 'the answer is no. In fact, if they hadn't been captured later, trying to rob the Overland Stage, I never would've known who they were. But while in jail, one of them bragged to another inmate how much fun they'd had raping and torturing Helen. He went into great detail, even describing how she'd begged and pleaded for her life, and the inmate ended up betraying them to the judge in exchange for a shorter sentence.'

Del Gardo shuddered. 'Please tell me they were hung, *senor*?'

'Unfortunately, yeah,' Coop said bitterly. 'I wished they'd been turned loose so I could personally pay them back for destroying my life. And they would've died real slow, believe me.'

There was a long painful silence.

Then Del Gardo buried his angst and said politely: 'I hope the soup is to your liking, *senor*. Despite these times of civil unrest, with bandits like Zapata and Heraclio Bernal raiding our ranches, the fact that we are still able to feed ourselves from our own fields is something I am most proud of.'

Coop tasted the cold corn chowder and nodded approvingly. 'I've never tasted better,' he said truthfully.

Del Gardo beamed. 'I hope you will feel the same way after you have tasted the pheasant. I shot it myself, this very morning.'

'He's one hell of a marksman,' Gospel told Coop. 'When he was younger he won a bunch of shooting medals while he was in the army. Ain't that right, Edwin?'

'I was lucky,' the Del Gardo said modestly. 'My father taught me well and — ' He broke off, alarmed by the sound of a single gunshot. It came from one of the bedrooms and instantly he looked horrified.

'*Madre de Dios*!' he exclaimed, and jumping up ran into the house.

'What the hell was that — *bandidos*?' Coop said as Gospel also jumped up.

Gospel grimly shook his head. 'That shot came from one of the girls' rooms — and Gabby's the only one here!' He hurried after Del Gardo, Coop right behind him.

14

Moments later, when the two of them burst into Gabriela's bedroom, they found it empty. But as they looked through the doorway leading to the adjoining bedroom, they saw Del Gardo kneeled on the floor cradling Gabriela in his arms. She was alive but unconscious and blood streamed from a bullet wound on her forehead.

Several concerned servants, including the manservant, stood huddled about them.

'I don't get it,' Gospel said as he and Coop entered the room. 'This is Sophia's bedroom. Why would Gabby shoot herself in here?' To the manservant, he added: 'Did you speak to the *senorita*?'

'No, *senor*. *Senorita* Gabriela, she was *inconsciente* when the *patron* found her!'

Triggered by the manservant's voice,

Del Gardo looked tearfully at Coop and Gospel. 'How could my daughter do such a thing? Does she not realize how much dishonor her suicide would cause our family?'

Coop started to reprimand the Don for his callous remark, but Gospel cut him off. 'Goddammit, never mind your family name, Edwin, just send someone to the village for a doctor!'

The distraught Don spoke through his tears. 'This I have already done, *mi amigo*. Dr. Cuevas should be here any moment.'

'While we're waiting for the doc,' Coop said, kneeling beside Gabriela, 'mind if I take a closer look at her, *senor*? I've had some experience with this type of wound.'

Del Gardo didn't answer. Overcome with distress, he clutched Gabriela even closer and broke down sobbing.

'*Patron*!' Gospel said, gripping the Don's shoulder. 'Get hold of yourself! Let Coop take a look at Gabby!'

Del Gardo stared blankly at him, as if

unable to grasp the situation. Then he numbly obeyed and loosened his hold on Gabriela.

Coop examined the two-inch gash on her forehead and saw that the bullet had only grazed the flesh, stunning Gabriela in the process. And though the self-inflicted wound was bleeding profusely, it was not life-threatening, and Coop knew Gabriela would recover with nothing more than a bad headache and a small scar. Greatly relieved, he turned to Gospel, saying: 'Get me some water and a cloth, *compadre*.'

'Sure thing . . . ' Gospel went to the nightstand, poured water from a jug into a small basin, grabbed a washcloth and came hurrying back.

Coop wetted the cloth and pressed it firmly against Gabriela's wound. He did this several times, each time squeezing the blood from the wet cloth into the basin before replacing it on her wound. It took a few minutes, but gradually the bleeding slowed and then stopped altogether . . . bringing a collective sigh of relief.

Slowly, Gabriela began to regain consciousness. Eyes still closed, she moaned softly. Her lips parted as if to speak, but no words came out. She moaned again and then stirred as if waking from a deep sleep. Her eyes fluttered open and she gazed blankly about her.

Elated, Del Gardo rushed to his daughter's side, intending to embrace her.

But Coop held him back. 'Wait, senor! Give her time to recover.'

'He's right,' Gospel said. 'Don't rush things or Gabby could pass out again.'

'*Si, si, mi amigo,*' Del Gardo said. 'You are right. I wait.'

Just then, Gabriela tried to move her head.

'No, no, lie still,' Coop said. 'The doctor's on his way. Stay quiet till he gets here.'

Gabriela seemed to understand. The fear left her eyes and she grew calm. She then looked about her, trying to focus. But her eyes wouldn't obey. She kept trying and after several minutes, she won the battle and her wandering gaze settled on her father.

At first she didn't grasp why he was so upset. Her eyes glazed as she searched her mind for answers. Then her thoughts finally gelled and everything came rushing back to her. 'Oh, papa,' she said, dismayed, 'I am so sorry . . .'

'No, no, do not be,' he replied. 'I am the one who should be sorry, not you. Nor your sisters, either. This is all my fault. If I hadn't been so possessive, I . . .' He paused as she drifted off, then he looked at Coop. 'My beloved Gabriela — you think she will be all right, *senor?*'

'Sure,' Coop said. 'So long as we keep her calm till the doc' gets here, she'll be fine.'

Del Gardo shook his head in despair. 'To think that I drove her to do such an awful thing devastates me. I should be punished . . . horse-whipped for my sins.'

'Easy, *senor*,' Coop said. 'If Gabriela sees you upset, it'll only upset her and that's the last thing we want.'

'Besides,' said Gospel, 'this ain't all your fault, Edwin. No matter what else you done, you didn't put the gun to her head or pull the trigger.'

'I might as well have,' Del Gardo said miserably. 'So many times you have told me not to be so strict with my daughters. But I refused to listen . . . to believe you . . . '

As if hearing her father's voice, Gabriela suddenly opened her eyes. She seemed stronger and smiled weakly at him. 'Do not worry, papa,' she whispered. 'I promise you, I will never scare you like this again!'

'That is good to hear,' he wept, 'because I could not live without you, my child.'

'Or I you, papa,' Gabriela replied. She closed her eyes, exhausted by her effort to talk, and drifted off again.

Del Gardo stared devotedly at her. 'May the Madonna be my witness,' he told Coop and Gospel, 'once my precious Gabriela recovers, I will never give her another reason to try to take her life or be unhappy in any way.'

'Reckon that's the best idea you ever had,' Gospel said.

'You won't be sorry, either,' Coop added. 'Losing a loved one is too painful to describe. Meanwhile, let's get her to bed, so she can rest till the doc arrives.'

'*Si, si*, of course,' Del Gardo said. 'If you will come with me, *por favor?*' Rising, he waited for Coop to gently scoop up Gabriela and then led him into her bedroom.

15

By the time Dr. Cuevas arrived, Gabriela had regained consciousness and was fully aware of her surroundings. She was still suffering from mild dizzy spells and a painful headache, but she never complained. She knew she had flirted with death and gotten away with it and the thought frightened her.

She looked at Coop, who was keeping vigil beside her bed, and found comfort in the tall gunfighter's presence. She squeezed his hand and smiled gratefully at him. He smiled back and mouthed one word: 'Rest.'

Gabriela nodded and closed her eyes.

Del Gardo, who was talking Gospel, noticed the way Coop and Gabriela looked at each other and frowned, as if disturbed.

Shortly, the manservant brought the doctor into the bedroom. Del Gardo introduced Dr. Cuevas to Coop and Gospel and explained what had happened. The doctor listened without interrupting. A soft-spoken, snowy-haired man of sixty, he quickly asserted himself by insisting that everyone leave while he examined Gabriela.

He then removed the wet towel from her forehead and examined her wound. Then, satisfied it was superficial he applied salve and bandaged her head. A compassionate man, he sensed Gabriela was struggling to get past the shock of almost killing herself and couldn't leave without supporting her. Grasping her hand, he smiled and in a fatherly tone, said: 'Do you know what I told your mother when I delivered you?'

Gabriela shook her head.

'I told her that I'd delivered many babies over the years, and they were all special to me. But you, I said, were extra special. And when she asked me why, I said because you were an angel, loaned to us by heaven, to bring joy and happiness to everyone.'

'I don't believe you,' Gabriela said, embarrassed. 'You're just saying that to make me feel better.'

'No, no, it's true, my child.'

'Why would you ever say something like that?'

'Because it is how I felt. And so did your mother, once she held you in her arms.'

Gabriela sighed regretfully. 'Too bad papa does not feel the same way. No matter how hard I try, I can never please him.'

'The fault is not yours,' Dr. Cuevas assured her. 'It lies with your father. Despite all his power and money, he is insecure and needy.'

'Papa — needy?' Gabriela scoffed. 'Oh, no, doctor. You're mistaken. My father doesn't need anyone!'

'We all need someone, little one. And Edwin is no exception. I know. I grew up with him. And I can assure you, my child, he's always been needy. That's why he was so devastated when he learned of your mother's infidelity. She had always been his lifeline to happiness. Her strength was his strength. Her courage was his courage. And her loving support made him feel invincible. Then her unfaithfulness crushed him. As did her sudden death. It forced him to realize that there were some things even he could not control. He would never admit this, of course, not even to himself. Instead, he became more determined to control everything, especially those he loved, in order to keep them near him.'

'But if that's true,' said Gabriela, 'why did he send my sisters away?'

Dr. Cuevas shrugged. 'I cannot say. Your father has never told me his reason. But if I were to guess, it was because he'd lost control of them. Once he realized they would always defy him, it was too much to tolerate. So he sent them to the convent . . . which is very sad, because Edwin has brought much pain to everyone . . . himself most of all.'

Gabriela absorbed the doctor's explanation in tight-lipped silence.

'So, what am I supposed to do?' she asked finally. 'I love papa dearly and I don't want to run away like my sisters tried to do. But at the same time I don't want to stay here and be his prisoner . . . '

'That's understandable. And you are right not to run away. Running away never solved anything.'

'But what other choice do I have?'

'Be patient with him, Gabriela. Be patient and understanding, without being submissive, and hopefully one day he will find inner peace and maturity. Once that happens he won't be afraid of losing you — which right now terrifies him. Instead he will learn to trust and respect you and therefore not have to treat you like a prisoner.'

'I hope you're right. Otherwise . . . ' Gabriela left the rest unsaid but there was no doubting her meaning.

'Let us hope it never comes to that,' Dr. Cuevas said, adding: 'I must go now. But first, promise me that you will stay in bed for the next few days and get plenty of rest.'

'*Lo prometo*, doctor.'

'And when you are finally strong enough to get up, do not do anything strenuous.'

'The way my head feels right now, doctor, just breathing feels too strenuous.'

'Rest will cure that,' Dr. Cuevas assured her. 'It will also prevent a relapse that could endanger your life. Meanwhile, before I go, there is something I must know.'

'Why did I shoot myself?'

'*Si.*'

'I didn't, doctor — at least, not deliberately. I was looking in a drawer for a bracelet that Sophia borrowed before she left and beside her jewelry box was a pistol — '

'Your sister owns a pistol?' Dr. Cuevas said, surprised.

'*Si.* Unlike me or Isabel, Sophia loves guns. She loves shooting them too. It was the one thing that she and papa had in common. In fact, they used to go hunting together.'

'This I never knew,' Dr. Cuevas said.

'That's because papa kept it a secret. Unlike most fathers, who would be proud of their daughter for being such a fine shot, his only concern was for the dignity of our family name. And even though he enjoyed Sophia's company, he decided hunting was not ladylike, so when she grew older he stopped taking her.'

'How sad. It might have helped bring them closer together.'

'It would have. Once, in confidence, Sophia said as much. As for shooting myself, doctor, it was just a silly mistake. When I picked up the gun I accidentally pulled the trigger and it went off . . . ' Gabriela paused, her hand absently straying to her bandaged forehead. 'I felt like I'd been hit with a hammer. Everything went dark and the next thing I remembered, I was on the floor in Sophia's bedroom in papa's arms.'

'I'm glad to hear this,' Dr. Cuevas

said, relieved. 'When I was told about the shooting — '

'You thought I'd tried to kill myself?'

'Such a thought did cross my mind, *si*.'

'Shame on you,' Gabriela scolded. 'You should know me better than that. I would *never* do such a blasphemous thing. It is sinful to take a life, even your own, and I would never do anything to destroy God's faith in me.'

Dr. Cuevas looked chagrined. 'You are right, *carina*. I should've had more faith in you. I'm sorry. Forgive me?'

'Of course.'

'*Gracias*.' Dr. Arbaca bent close and kissed Gabriela on the forehead. 'I must go now. But I will look in on you again later in the week. Meanwhile, rest, rest, rest.'

Gabriela nodded and watched as he picked up his bag and left the room. She then laid her head back on the pillow with a troubled sigh . . .

16

Dr. Cuevas found Del Gardo, Coop and Gospel drinking *tequila* at the bar on the torch-lit terrace, anxiously awaiting his diagnosis. He quickly assured Del Gardo that he needn't worry about Gabriela. She was fine. As long as her wound was kept clean and she didn't overexert herself, she could go about her daily routine and not have to worry about a relapse. He then repeated his promise to return in a few days to verify that she was recovering, wished everyone goodnight and drove off in his buggy.

Gospel, seated between Coop and Del Gardo, hooted joyfully and punched the air. 'Goddammit, if this ain't a reason to celebrate, I don't know what is!'

'You're right!' Coop exclaimed. He sucked on a slice of lime, raised his glass and toasted: 'To Gabriela!'

Gospel and Del Gardo clinked

glasses, 'Amen,' and drank.

Del Gardo then excused himself, saying he was exhausted and had many things to do tomorrow. 'Before I go, though,' he said to Coop, 'may I ask a favor of you?'

'Name it.'

'Naturally, you will be my guest tonight, but is it also possible for you to remain here for a few more days?'

'And do what?'

'It is not so much *what* you will do,' Del Gardo said, 'but more what your presence will do.'

'What's he's trying to say,' said Gospel, 'is that just by being here, you'll help Gabby get better faster.'

'In other words,' Coop said to Del Gardo, 'you want me to keep her company?'

'*Si* — if that would not be too inconvenient?'

'Not at all,' Coop said. 'Be my pleasure. But I am curious — why me?'

Del Gardo smiled knowingly. 'Because I have seen the way Gabriela looks at you and, if you'll forgive me, how you look at her.'

'Whoa, wait a minute,' Coop said, 'if you're suggesting — '

'No, no,' exclaimed Del Gardo, 'do not even consider such ugly thoughts, *hombre*. We have only just met, but I trust you as if you were my son. No, what I'm trying to say is, due to the continual disobedience of my other daughters, I've been forced to let my affairs lapse. And now, if I were to spend time giving Gabriela the proper care she needs while she recuperates, it would only delay me further. Do you understand?'

Before Coop could reply, Gospel suddenly doubled over and grabbed his abdomen as pain shot through his right side. It only lasted for a few seconds but he broke out in a cold sweat. Then he straightened up, wiped his brow and grinned wickedly at Coop.

'In case you ain't aware of it, *amigo*, I've also seen how Gabby looks at you. And believe me, it's all hearts and flowers.'

Coop shrugged, convinced. 'Okay, if you say so,' he said.

'There is something else to consider,'

Del Gardo said. 'While you are here with Gabriela, *senor*, we will have time to discuss my plans for the next robbery.'

'Fair enough,' Coop said. 'I'd planned on making dust in the morning, but I reckon a few more days can't hurt.'

Del Gardo smiled, relieved. 'I promise you will not regret your decision. Now, if you'll forgive me, *mi amigos*, I will say goodnight and see you at breakfast.' With a polite nod, he entered the house.

'Sonofabitch,' Gospel said, grinning at Coop. 'If you ain't one sneaky coyote.'

'Meaning?'

'For months now, I been trying to find a good reason to stick around so I could throw a rope over Sophia and never once come close — while you, without even trying, end up with the Don asking you to keep his favorite daughter company. I mean, Judas, talk about stepping in a prairie pancake and not getting your shit-kickers dirty!'

Coop chuckled. 'Eloquence . . . thy name is Gospel Curtis!'

17

For the next few days Coop kept his word and spent most of his waking hours with Gabriela. As her father had predicted, his company stopped her from feeling lonely or depressed, and enabled her to endure the monotonous boredom of resting in bed. But by the third morning she could no longer stand being bedridden any longer. Despite the beseeching of her personal maid, Gabriela bathed, dressed and was already seated at the terrace table when Coop came to breakfast.

'Don't you dare scold me,' she warned before he could say anything. 'I feel fine. My dizziness is gone and so is my headache — well, almost anyway.'

'I'm glad to hear that,' Coop said.

'You don't sound glad. You sound like you think I should still be in bed!'

'Well, I'm no sawbones, but I do

remember what the doc said: don't overdo things or you could have a relapse.'

'Eating breakfast is hardly 'overdoing' things,' Gabriela said. 'I mean my wound's almost healed and even papa said it was all right. Please don't be angry with me,' she added. 'I feel gloomy enough without you scowling at me.'

'Fair enough,' Coop said. 'No more scowling. I ain't angry anyways. I just don't want anything to happen to you because you didn't get enough rest.'

'Nothing's going to happen to me,' Gabriela promised. 'Or you. We're going to have a grand life together. Aren't we?' she said when he didn't reply. 'I mean, you do like being here with me, don't you?'

' . . . Sure.'

'Then why did you hesitate?'

'Hesitate?'

'Yes, just now. I asked you if you liked being here and you hesitated.'

'If I did,' Coop said, 'I wasn't aware of it. Reckon your question surprised me.'

'Why? For the past few days you've looked after me, kept me company and even made it clear that you cared for me.'

'I do.'

'And I've certainly tried to show how much I care for you.'

'No argument there.'

'So why were you surprised? I wouldn't be if you'd asked me the same question.'

Coop shrugged. 'What can I say, Gabriela? I just was and that's all there is to it. Besides,' he added, 'what difference does it make whether I hesitated or not? I must want to be here or I would've left, like I intended and that would've been the end of it. But I didn't. I chose to stay.'

'Yes, but for how long? I mean, do you plan to ride on — eventually?'

'Eventually?' Coop chewed on the word and then shrugged. 'Reckon that's one of them words I can't hang my hat on. It's like never or forever. A fella's got to be either a fool or a liar if he makes that kind of promise.'

His words stung and Gabriela felt rejected. 'Papa was right about you, after all.'

'In what way?'

'He warned me not to get attached to you. Said, once a drifter always a drifter. But I didn't believe him. I thought you . . . we . . . had something special.'

'We do.'

'Then why won't you commit?'

'Commit to what?'

'Us, of course!'

Coop sighed, exasperated. 'Gabriela, we've only known each other for a short time . . . much too short a time to be making commitments. Besides, I'm old enough to be your father — ' He broke off as she burst into tears, jumped up and ran indoors.

'Wait!' he called after her. 'Gabriela, please . . . '

She ignored him and stormed off into her bedroom.

Frustrated, he threw down his napkin and glared at the food before him.

'Mister,' he told himself, 'if you're half as smart as you think you are, you'll saddle up and get the hell out of here! And I mean now!'

There was a long silence that was finally broken by the howl of a lonely coyote.

'Shut up,' Coop told it. 'Keep your damned opinion to yourself!'

The coyote stopped howling. Silence returned.

Then someone chuckled behind him. 'Got you talking to yourself now, has she?'

Coop whirled around and saw Gospel grinning at him from the doorway.

'Dammit, how long you been standing there?'

'Long enough to know you're neck-deep in trouble.'

'Thanks for the encouraging words,' Coop said sourly.

'You know me, *amigo*. No matter how ugly it gets, I always got your back.'

'That's what worries me.'

126

Gospel laughed. 'Now you're getting smart.' Approaching the table, he picked up a tortilla from one of the plates and began spreading guacamole and hot sauce on it. 'I don't know what you're bitching about anyways. Most fellas I know would sell their ranch to have a pretty gal like Gabriela chasing them.'

'I wouldn't blame them,' Coop said. 'But — '

'I know, I know, you ain't ready to settle down yet.'

'I settled down once before. It didn't end up too well.'

'Yeah, but this time might be different. You like Gabby. And there's no doubt she loves you. Hell, you'd only have to snap your fingers and she'd jump to be your wife.'

'I had a wife, remember? And in here,' Coop said, pointing at his heart, 'I've still got one.'

'Maybe so,' said Gospel. 'But memories can't warm your bed at night. For that, you need a real woman — a woman like Gabriela. Hell, she ain't only prettier than a spring colt, she's rich. And when her old man dies, she'll be even richer and so will the gent she's hitched to.'

If Coop heard Gospel, he didn't show it. A faraway look entered his flint-gray eyes and he said: 'Know what's ironic? I got no one to blame for this mess but myself.'

'How you figure that?'

'I should've ridden on, right from the start. I should've obeyed my gut instinct and told Del Gardo, thanks but no thanks, and left.'

'But you didn't,' Gospel reminded. 'And that should tell you something. For a confirmed loner like you, hell, it would be only natural to turn down his offer. And to be honest, *amigo*, I was as surprised as a plucked chicken when you didn't.'

'Not as surprised as me,' Coop admitted. His mind wandered unhappily before he continued. 'You know, since the day I lost Helen and started drifting, I always took it for granted that I'd never find another woman like her. She was perfect for me. And no other woman could hope to top that. Hell, she'd be a fool to even try.' He paused, his mind painfully dwelling on his dead wife. 'Besides, even if by some rare fluke I *did* find another woman to roost with, who's to say she'd want me? Jesus, I'm no prize catch. I mean, what decent woman would be fool enough to marry a gunfighter, a drifter with no roots and nothing to offer? My God, she'd have to be *loco*.'

'Not if her name's Gabriela,' Gospel said.

'But she's still a child.'

'Some child!'

'And even if she weren't and we both wanted to get married, Del Gardo would never approve of me as a son-in-law. I wouldn't expect him to, either. Or blame him. Hell, in his shoes, I'd tell me to get the hell off my ranch and never come back!'

'The Don would never do that.

You're too valuable to him. We both are!'

'Because of this robbery he's got planned?'

'Of course! Why do you think he went out of his way to recruit you?'

'Recruit — what're you talking about?'

'When you first came into the Holy Moses, he liked the way you handled Ezra Foley and decided you were the man to help me rob the Gold Train.'

'Gold Train?' Coop said, puzzled. 'What Gold Train? Come on, *compadre*,' he insisted when Gospel didn't reply. 'Spit it out.'

'Sorry, *amigo*. I can't — '

'Jesus,' Coop exclaimed as it suddenly hit him. 'Del Gardo's already told you everything about the robbery, hasn't he?'

'Hell, no, I — '

'Don't lie!' Coop exclaimed. 'And don't play dumb either. It ain't your style.'

Gospel hung his head. 'Okay,' he

admitted. 'You're right. He did fill me in on it.'

'Then, spill. Come clean.'

'If I do, *amigo*, you got to promise me something.'

'What?'

'You got to swear that when Del Gardo gets around to telling you about robbing the Gold Train, you'll pretend to be surprised. Otherwise, I ain't saying another word.'

'I swear,' Coop said. 'Now, talk to me, dammit.'

18

The railroad bridge spanning Deep River Gorge was built by Confederate engineers near the end of the Civil War in a desperate attempt to supply their troops that were pinned down by superior Union forces in the hills bordering Texas and New Mexico. As history shows, it was too little, too late, and the only thing that saved the ragtag rebel army from being slaughtered was General Robert E. Lee's timely surrender.

With the war over, and the mustered-out soldiers on both sides only too happy to limp home, the need for this particular spur ended and the trains stopped running. Weeds grew over the rusting tracks and the wooden trestle bridge began to rot.

But now, almost thirty years later, numerous small towns had sprung up along the border and countless settlers were arriving daily, all in need of supplies. As a result the Texas-New Mexico & Arizona railroad — designated TNM&A — was again needed. Hundreds of Gandy Dancers, as the workers were called, were hired to repair the tracks and the trestle bridge and soon trains from both directions rumbled across it.

Monthly, one such train carried the payrolls for troops stationed at the various posts and forts in New Mexico and Arizona. On occasion, it also carried gold bullion that connecting railroads transported to the Denver mint. This made the train an enticing target for border bandits, and its departure from El Paso was kept secret. It was also heavily guarded by soldiers, all of whom remained hidden inside the boxcars until the train was on its way. From then on, their visible presence as they sat on the roofs of the boxcars was enough to discourage bandits and so far, the Gold Train, as it was nicknamed had never been robbed.

But this morning, before the sun had burned off the cool desert mist, Coop and Gospel planned on ending that streak. Based on information that Don Del Gardo had acquired by bribing a railroad official, the Gold Train was leaving El Paso at dawn and was scheduled to reach Deep River Gorge shortly after ten o'clock.

Coop and Gospel arrived at the bridge two hours prior to that. They were escorted by Col. Abelardo and his *vaqueros*, who kept watch from the tops of the sand dunes while the two gunmen climbed down the trestle supporting the bridge and tied bundles of dynamite to the beams directly under the tracks. It was precarious work. One slip meant they would drop two hundred feet into the river at the bottom of the gorge. There, even if by some miracle the fall didn't kill them, the tumultuous rapids would sweep them downriver over a towering waterfall onto the rocks below.

Gospel seemed unfazed by his possible fate. He hummed cheerfully to himself as he handled his share of the dynamite. But Coop, leery of heights, battled his nerves. He forced himself to not look down and worked in grim tight-lipped silence. Even so, despite the chilling wind, he was sweating profusely by the time he'd tied the last of the dynamite in place and quickly started climbing up the trestle to the tracks.

'Hey, wait for me!' Gospel yelled.

Coop ignored him. He didn't stop climbing until he reached the top and felt solid ground underfoot. Then he leaned against the rocks and sighed with relief.

'What the hell's your rush?' Gospel asked as he joined him. 'The train ain't due for another hour or so.'

'I had to take a piss,' Coop lied, 'and didn't feel like doing it where the wind could blow it back in my face!'

Gospel chuckled — then suddenly doubled over, grimacing as pain knifed through his belly. The attack was worse than usual and Gospel dropped the spool of wire he was holding, staggered and almost fell.

Coop grabbed his arm, steadying him. 'You okay?' he asked when the blond-haired gunman finally straightened up.

'Yeah, yeah . . . I'm fine . . . '

He was anything but fine, but Coop knew it was useless to argue with him and kept quiet.

Gospel massaged his sore groin for a few moments and then picked up his spool of wire. 'C'mon, *amigo*, let's get this over with.'

Together, the two gunmen started walking backward, each holding a spool of wire, the ends of which were attached to the bundles of dynamite tied to the trestle. As they walked, the wire slowly unraveled and by the time they had reached their hiding place behind a rocky outcrop, the spools were almost empty. Ducking out of sight, they kneeled beside a detonator box.

Using pliers, they clipped off the ends of the wires, stripped away the outer coating and wound the bare wires around two copper terminals atop the box. Gospel then pulled up the handle controlling the firing mechanism and nodded to Coop, who signaled to Col. Abelardo that all was ready.

'See anything yet?' Gospel yelled to him.

'*Nada, senor! Es demasiado pronto!*'

'Well, don't go to sleep,' Gospel said. 'The train could be early, you know?'

'Early or late, *gringo*,' Col. Abelardo replied haughtily, 'I shall not fail to alert you.' He turned his back on Gospel and continued glassing the horizon.

'Arrogant pig,' Gospel growled to Coop. 'You were right, *amigo*. I should've plugged that sonofabitch long ago.'

'First, let's blow the bridge and get the gold,' said Coop. 'After that, I'll be happy to shoot the bastard myself.'

Time crawled by. Minutes seemed like hours and the sun had grown uncomfortably hot by the time a spiral of black smoke appeared on the eastern horizon. Col. Abelardo spotted it through his field glasses and signaled to Gospel and Coop that the train was approaching. He and his *vaqueros* then scrambled down from the sand dunes and took up positions behind the rocks alongside the tracks.

Twenty minutes later the ground underfoot began to tremble, indicating that the locomotive and its long string of boxcars were nearing the sand dunes. Here, the tracks made a sharp right-hand bend, forcing trains to slow down before reaching the long straightaway that led across the bridge.

Gospel grinned at Coop, spat on his palms and grasped the handle, ready to push it down when the Gold Train appeared. Earlier they had done some mental arithmetic and concluded that once the bridge was blown and the startled engineer had hopefully applied the brakes, the slow-moving freight train would still need the entire length of the straightaway in order to stop before plunging into the gorge.

Timing was crucial. If the bridge was destroyed too soon, the engineer would be able to stop the train while it was still near the sand dunes, allowing the soldiers to take cover and fight off their attackers; alternately, if Gospel waited too long to destroy the bridge, the engineer wouldn't have time to stop the train and it would plunge into the river. Once that happened, the boxcars would be swept away by the churning rapids eliminating any chance of recovering the gold or the payroll.

Underfoot the shaking increased as the Gold Train rumbled closer.

Coop peered around the rocks in the direction of the bend. Another anxious minute passed . . . then finally the train came steaming around the sand dunes. Heart thudding, Coop waited until the black locomotive with its garish red-painted wheels approached the start of the long straightaway and then gave Gospel a thumbs up.

Gospel vigorously wound the side-handle a few times, priming the charge, and then pushed down plunger on the detonator box.

Instantly the dynamite tied to the trestle exploded with a thunderous roar, blowing the bridge sky-high. The huge explosion also ripped up the tracks spanning the bridge, as well as the mangled rails stretching out from both sides of the gorge!

Coop and Gospel, along with Col. Abelardo and the *vaqueros*, flattened themselves against the rocks as debris rained down around them.

Simultaneously, in the cab of the locomotive the veteran, quick-thinking engineer recovered from the shock of the bridge exploding and grabbed the brake lever. He pulled it toward him, engaging the brakes. A shrill screeching followed as locked-up steel wheels skidded on steel rails.

The explosion, followed by the abrupt slow-down, caught the startled troopers by surprise. They were all thrown off the roofs of the boxcars. Many of them were killed or injured by the fall, while the rest were badly shaken up.

Meanwhile, the skidding locomotive was gradually slowing down, but not fast enough to save it from falling into the gorge. Adding to the oncoming carnage, the brakes on the rest of the train were not capable of responding as rapidly. As a result the caboose and the rear boxcars slammed into the cars ahead, derailing them so that they jumped the tracks and plowed into the ground.

But out of disaster came a much-needed miracle. Having to drag the damaged, freight-loaded boxcars over the dirt and rocks helped to slow down the train, enabling the still-skidding locomotive to finally stop within a few feet of the edge of the gorge.

19

As soon as the train ground to a halt, Coop and Gospel darted out from behind the rocks and sprinted to the derailed boxcar that was linked to the damaged caboose. Though the car was unmarked, they knew from Del Gardo's informant that it not only carried the U.S. mail but more importantly, also the gold bullion and payroll money.

Col. Abelardo, on seeing Coop and Gospel take off, waved his saber and led his *vaqueros* in a charge against the soldiers who were still alive. Earlier, the arrogant Colonel had assured Del Gardo that the surviving troopers would quickly surrender. He was wrong. The veteran soldiers crawled behind the corpses of their comrades and bravely fought back. Their withering fire surprised the attacking *vaqueros*, killing several and forcing the others to retreat and find cover themselves.

Coop and Gospel ignored the shoot-out. Ducked low, they continued sprinting to the derailed boxcar. They drew their guns as they got close to the wreckage, but no one was alive to challenge them. Picking their way through the dead troopers sprawled around them, they cautiously approached the mail car, which lay on its side near the buckled railroad tracks. They reached it unscathed. But as they went to look inside, they heard someone groan nearby. They turned and saw the old caboose driver, his body crumpled and bleeding among the rocks. He was barely alive. He stared at them with bloodshot eyes and in a hoarse whisper begged them to shoot him.

Coop, feeling sorry for the old-timer, grudgingly shot him in the head.

'Don't feel bad,' Gospel said. 'Hell, you'd do the same for a dog, wouldn't you?'

'Some comfort,' Coop growled and turned back to the derailed mail car.

Gospel joined him. Together, they

peered through the splintered side-panel and saw two corpses by the mail sacks. Both wore U.S. Deputy Marshal badges and Coop and Gospel realized they were the guards, who'd been killed during the derailment.

At the rear of the car was a large cast-iron safe. Though overturned it was still intact and they knew opening it would be tough. They had expected Del Gardo's informant to give them the combination, but he'd claimed it was known by only two men: the bank manager in El Paso responsible for shipping the payroll money and the gold bullion and the government official awaiting its delivery at the Denver Mint.

'C'mon, *amigo*,' Gospel said cheerfully. 'Let's get to work!' He pulled a bundle of dynamite from inside his jacket, kicked the splintered boards apart and squeezed between them into the car. Coop followed him.

They crawled past the dead guards to the safe. Gospel gave it a kiss. 'Be a good girl now, honey. Open up for Uncle Curtis, so we can all live like millionaires!'

'Come on, come on,' Coop grumbled as outside the gunfire increased. 'Will you quit messing around and blow the goddamn thing!'

Gospel chuckled, unfazed by the raging shootout, and taped a stick of dynamite to each hinge on the door of the safe. He then inserted the fuses, took a match from his pocket, flared it on his thumbnail and lit each fuse. They burned quickly and Gospel scrambled after Coop, who was already squeezing between the broken woodwork.

Once outside, they sprinted for the rocks.

They never made it.

They were still a few steps from cover when the dynamite exploded. The blast not only demolished the mail boxcar, but hit Coop and Gospel from behind like a giant punch in the back, slamming them to the ground. Dazed, they lay there, hands clasped over their heads as debris rained down on them.

The destruction of the mail boxcar demoralized the six remaining troopers. They saw the damaged safe lying by the railroad tracks, where the blast had blown it, and realizing they had failed to protect it, decided to save their lives and ceased firing. One soldier tied a kerchief to his rifle and waved it in surrender. Col. Abelardo brandished his saber in acknowledgement and ordered his *vaqueros* to round up the prisoners.

Once the debris stopping raining down on them, Coop and Gospel scrambled to the safe. It lay on its back, and as they got close they saw that its door had been blown off.

Both whooped exuberantly.

But their elation was short-lived. The safe was empty!

Crushed, they looked around, expecting to see the ground littered with greenbacks and gold bars. Again they were disappointed. There was only scattered debris.

'Sonofabitch!' Gospel cursed. 'The bastards outfoxed us!'

'Yeah, but how?'

'Beats me. But . . . wait, wait . . . it's got to be the informant. He must've sold out.'

'Why the hell would he do that?' said Coop. 'By double-crossing Del Gardo, he cost himself his share of the gold. Unless . . . '

'Unless what, *amigo*?'

'He played it straight with us and got outsmarted by someone he didn't figure on.'

'Like, who?'

'I don't know. The bank manager in El Paso, most likely. He must've suspected the informant and decided to test this fella's integrity with a dry run.'

'Makes sense,' Gospel agreed. He shook his head in disgust. 'I should've listened to my pa. Never trust a goddamn banker, he said. They'll piss on you every chance they — ' He broke off as rifle fire crackled behind them.

Whirling around, they saw the bodies of the surrendered troopers sprawled on the ground. Facing them was a firing squad made up of *vaqueros*. Lowering their rifles, they stood at attention, awaiting their next orders from Col. Abelardo.

Enraged, Coop aimed his carbine at the arrogant officer. 'I ought to kill you, you murdering bastard!'

'Execution is not murder,' Col. Abelardo sneered. 'These dead pigs were rebels. As a soldier, it was my duty to shoot them.'

'But they were under a white flag!'

'The rules of war do not apply to rebel dogs!'

'Then why'd you let them surrender?'

'I did not let them, *Yanqui*! It was their choice!' The Colonel spat contemptuously on the nearest corpse. 'It is the choice of cowards! And cowards deserve to die.'

Gospel grinned, 'Damn' right they do,' and shot him.

The bullet punched a hole in the officer's chest. He gasped, mouth agape, eyes wide with shock, and then collapsed, dead before he hit the ground.

The startled *vaqueros* quickly aimed their rifles at Coop and Gospel, ready to shoot. But none of them pulled the trigger. They were so accustomed to obeying commands, without an order from their leader they couldn't decide if they should shoot or not.

Coop decided for them. Firing three quick shots in the dirt at their feet, he yelled: 'Go back to your homes, *hombres*! Go on! *Vamos*!' he added when they didn't move. '*Salir de la mierda de aqui*!'

The *vaqueros* hesitated and looked questioningly at one another. Momentarily, they were uncertain about obeying a *gringo*. Then they nodded in silent agreement, lowered their rifles, mounted their horses and rode back toward the border . . . and to their fields that needed planting

20

It was late afternoon that same day when Coop and Gospel finally reached Rocas Rojas. It had been a long hot sweaty ride and both gunmen were played out and testy. Dismounting outside the Holy Moses, they hitched their equally weary horses to the rail, slapped the trail dust from their clothes and entered the dilapidated saloon.

Inside, they paused by the door and warily surveyed the noisy smoke-filled room. Nothing had changed. The place was packed with the usual rowdy crowd. The bar-girls were busy luring their eager customers upstairs, the bartenders were serving watered-down whiskey to the drunks, and at the gaming tables the gamblers were happily fleecing the poker players out of their hard-earned gold dust.

'Poor dumb bastards,' Gospel said as

he and Coop pushed through the crowd toward the bar. 'They never learn, do they? I mean, no one can beat a stacked deck.'

'Don't tell *them* that,' Coop said. 'It would ruin their dreams.'

'They wouldn't believe me anyway.'

'Why should they? Hell, every day they beat the odds just by *finding* gold, so why wouldn't they think they could beat these dealers? Besides,' Coop added as one of the players won a hand and gleefully brandished his cards, 'win or lose, look how much fun they're having.'

They had reached the bar. The tall bartender, having seen them coming, pushed two drunken miners aside to make room for the gunmen. He then poured two tequilas, set them on the bar and left the bottle.

'Nothing like good service,' Gospel grinned, reaching for his drink, 'especially when the price is right.'

'Amen!' Coop tossed back his tequila and glanced up at the gallery, wondering where Lorna was.

'Don't waste your bullets here, *amigo*,' Gospel told him 'There are clean sheets waiting elsewhere for you — ' he stopped, grabbed his groin and doubled over in pain.

Coop grasped his arm, steadying him, and waited for Gospel to straighten up. But this time the handsome yellow-haired gunman remained bent over, gasping as another agonizing pain knifed through his lower abdomen. He fought the pain for as long as he could, then crumpled to the floor and lay there, groaning.

Some of the customers saw Gospel collapse and quickly gathered around.

'Get back!' Coop shouted. 'Go on! Get back, damn you!' He kneeled beside Gospel and gently rolled his friend over. Gospel's normally tanned face had turned ash-gray and was bathed in sweat. 'Rest easy,' Coop told him. 'I'll get the doc'.'

Gospel was in too much pain to hear him. He writhed around on the floor . . . until finally, overwhelmed by pain, he mercifully fainted.

Coop turned to the crowd and barked: 'One of you go fetch the doc! Hurry!'

'You heard him!' Lorna said as she elbowed her way through the crowd. 'Free drinks for the first one of you who gets Dr. Simms!'

It was all the incentive the miners needed. Several of them bolted to the door, fighting each other in their eagerness to get outside.

Lorna kneeled beside Gospel and kissed him fondly on the forehead. 'Hang in there, Curtis,' she begged. 'The doc's coming . . . '

'He can't hear you,' Coop said grimly. 'He passed out.'

'Then we can't wait any longer! Can you carry him over to Dr. Simms' office?'

'Sure,' Coop said, picking Gospel up. 'Lead the way.'

Together, they pushed through the onlookers to the door. There, Coop stopped as Gospel suddenly opened his pain-filled eyes and tried to speak. But nothing came out.

'Don't talk, *compadre*,' Coop begged. 'Save your strength.'

Gospel refused to listen. Lips working with great effort, he fought to form words and this time, managed to find his voice. 'D-Don't be . . . damned fool,' he whispered hoarsely. 'She . . . G-Gabby . . . loves you . . . needs . . . you . . . and . . . ' His voice faded and his eyes glazed over as he lost consciousness.

'C'mon,' Lorna urged, holding the door open for Coop. 'Hurry!'

Coop started out — only to bump into a large, bulky, gray-haired man in a black suit, who carried a doctor's bag.

'Where do you think you're going?' he demanded.

'To the doctor's,' Coop replied.

'I *am* the doctor,' Dr. Harlan Simms said. 'Now, take this man back inside so I can examine him.' He brushed past Coop and stopped at the nearest empty table. 'This'll do. Put him down here!'

Coop gently placed Gospel on the table and stepped back beside Lorna, who was trying to restrain a bunch of bleary-eyed drunks and curious bar-girls.

Dr. Simms held his stethoscope to Gospel's chest, listened briefly then asked Coop: 'Before he passed out, what was wrong with him? I mean, were there any symptoms?'

'It's his belly, doc'. He keeps getting bad stabbing pains — '

'He's had them for a couple of weeks now,' Lorna added. 'I've been telling him to go see you, but he wouldn't listen to me.'

'To me, either,' said Coop. 'Sonofa-gun's too damned stubborn — '

'These pains?' Dr. Simms inter-rupted. 'Are they down here?' He pointed at the right side of Gospel's lower abdomen.

'Yeah. 'Least, that's where he always grabs himself.'

'Sounds like a ruptured appendix.'

'Jesus!'

'We must get him to my office right away! I need to operate. I warn you, though,' he said as Coop picked up Gospel's limp body. 'I'll do my damnedest to save your friend. But I'm no big-city surgeon, so don't get your hopes up until after the surgery.'

'Just do the best you can,' Coop said. 'That's all any man can do.'

21

But it wasn't to be.

Right after surgery Dr. Simms came out into the waiting room, where Coop and Lorna were anxiously pacing. Peeling off his rubber gloves, he grimly shook his head at them. 'I'm sorry. I'm afraid I couldn't save him.'

Lorna gave a tiny sob and tears flooded her eyes.

Dr. Simms gripped her shoulder comfortingly. 'I did everything I could, my dear, believe me. But he was too far gone.'

'Was it his — appendix?' Coop asked.

'Yes,' Dr. Simms said. 'I can't be sure, of course, but I'd say it ruptured yesterday or maybe the day before and, like you said, he's been fighting the pain ever since . . . '

'Damn,' Coop said softly.

'It's a lousy shame, I know — '

'Could you have saved him if we'd gotten him in here sooner?'

'You mean before his appendix burst?'

'Yeah.'

'I don't know. Like I said, I'm just a country doctor and most of my patients don't have to go under the knife. However, I do know this: it certainly would have given Mr. Curtis a better shot at surviving.' Dr. Simms paused and gave a long frustrated sigh. 'Nothing left to do now but notify the coroner.'

'I'll handle that,' Coop offered.

'All right,' Lorna agreed. 'But be sure to tell him I'll pay for Gospel's burial.'

'Will do,' Coop said.

'Then I'll see you later, okay?'

'Sure. After I've talked to the undertaker I'll come by for a drink.'

'Good . . . ' Lorna sniffed back her tears, turned and hurried out.

'How much do I owe you?' Coop asked Dr. Simms.

'Nothing. Miss Lorna already said she'd pay.'

'For the funeral, yeah, but — '

'Funeral — grave diggers — my services — it's all included in one price. Now, if you'll excuse me, Mr. Cooper, I'd like to start making arrangements for the body to be transferred to the coroner's office.'

Coop nodded, took one final, regretful look in the direction of the surgery and then started for the door.

'Oh, Mr. Cooper — hold up.'

Coop turned as the doctor approached, holding something out to him.

'I almost forget, son. Right before he went under, Mr. Curtis asked me to give you this.' He handed Coop a leather sheath containing Gospel's knife.

'Thanks,' Coop said, 'I appreciate that, doc.' He looked at the knife, remembering as he did that the last time he'd seen it was when Curtis had killed Foley with it. He then nodded goodbye to the doctor and walked out.

22

The next morning, shortly after sunup, Lorna paid two of her long-time customers to bury Gospel in the unfenced cemetery behind her saloon. The day before she'd also paid for a headstone bearing Gospel's name and the date he'd died. She'd wanted to include his date of birth, but neither she nor anyone else in town knew what it was, so she left a blank space in case she ever met someone who could tell her.

After leaving the stonemason, she'd gone to the mission and asked Father Ruiz to say a prayer for Gospel. But the gentle, soft-spoken padre's compassion only stretched so far. He explained that he did not condone gunmen who killed people for a living and couldn't ask God to forgive such evilness by accepting Gospel's soul into heaven.

Lorna was surprised by the padre's

lack of compassion. Coop wasn't. Nor was he surprised the next morning when he and Lorna were the only mourners at Gospel's grave. When it was his time to be buried in Boot Hill, he expected to die alone and without a mourner in sight.

'That's so sad,' Lorna said as she and Coop left the cemetery. 'To spend your entire life without making any friends, seems so . . . well, so pointless . . . so wasteful.'

'Reckon it comes with the territory.'

'What do you mean?'

'Not too many folks want to pal around with a gunfighter.'

'I suppose not. Doesn't that bother you, Coop?'

'Uh-uh. A hired gunny can't afford to have friends.'

'Why not?'

'Might come a day when he's paid to kill them. And it's hard enough on your conscience to gun down a stranger, without adding to your guilt by killing a pal.'

'If you feel guilty,' Lorna said, 'how come you keep doing it?'

'I got no choice.'

'Nonsense! There're other jobs you could do, if you wanted to.'

'Name one.'

'W-Well, you could punch cattle or — or work in a store or a saloon.'

'Oh, sure,' Coop said sourly. 'Who wouldn't want a gunfighter working for them? Come on in, folks! Buy your groceries here and risk being gunned down by some hot shot lawman or bounty hunter!'

'All right, point taken,' Lorna admitted. 'So you'd have to change your name and work in a place where they don't know you. It's still work, and anything would be better than — ' She stopped, realizing he wasn't listening.

He stood staring back at the cemetery as if seeing ghosts. And when he did finally speak, his voice came from far-off. 'That's why guilt is the perfect punishment. We all got to pay the price for what we do along the trail, there's no dodging that, no matter if you're good or bad.'

'I don't think you're bad, Coop.'

'You're prejudiced.'

'Please, don't joke. I'm serious.'

Realizing she was, Coop had no answer.

'At the same time, I'm not excusing what you do, either.'

Coop saw the love shining in her eyes and said wryly: 'Right now, you'd have a hard time convincing a judge of that.'

'I'm not talking to a judge,' Lorna said crossly. 'I'm talking to the man I love. And to him I'm saying, much as I hate what you do and can't condone it, at least you only kill men who deserve killing . . . men who are killers themselves.'

'And that justifies it?'

'No. I've already said it didn't. But right or wrong, it serves a purpose by ridding the world of murderers . . . and that can't be all bad. At least you aren't a hypocrite.'

'You got someone particular in mind?'

'Yes, most of the people I grew up with back east. They used to refer to folks living west of St. Louis as 'uncivilized'. As for the territories, they considered them to be the 'wild west' or the 'untamed frontier' and thought all Indians were savages.'

Coop shrugged indifferently. 'That's just ignorance talking.'

'It's also delusional. If these people would just look in the mirror occasionally they'd realize their way of life is no different — perhaps even worse.'

Her anger surprised Coop. 'Sounds like you're talking from personal experience.'

'I am . . . ' Lorna paused, gave a troubled sigh, and said: 'As a kid, growing up in the slums of Philly, I saw men and women robbed and murdered right in front of me. I mean it happened so often it became almost a common occurrence. And usually for reasons straight out of the Bible: power, greed, hate, jealousy — take your pick. What's worse, most of the victims were immigrants who barely spoke English, so there wasn't much they could do about it. So they accepted their lot because, as you just said, they believed it was the price they had to pay for enjoying the freedom that America promised them.'

'Some goddamn price,' Coop grumbled.

'Yes. But the irony is, compared to the cruelty and injustices most of them had to endure in Europe or Russia or wherever else they came from, it was worth it. To them, it was the lesser of two evils.'

'So two evils *do* make a right.'

'I'm not saying that. Nor am I saying that you or anyone else should be forgiven for taking another person's life — '

'Then what *are* you saying?'

Lorna hesitated, not sure herself. Finally, unable to find a satisfactory answer, she pressed against him, her face uplifted, her eyes begging him to kiss her.

He did, with all the passion he could summon.

Aroused, Lorna responded. The kiss lasted until they were out of breath. And when they finally broke apart, she smiled at him, content and satisfied.

He smiled back.

But as they continued on toward her saloon, Coop didn't share Lorna's feelings. He knew she wasn't the woman who could make him quit drifting. But, not wanting to hurt her, he took the coward's way out and kept quiet.

On reaching the rear of the Holy Moses, Coop opened the back door for Lorna but didn't accompany her inside.

'Aren't you coming in for a drink?' she said.

'Maybe later.'

'You're lying,' she said. 'I can see it in your eyes. You're pulling out, aren't you?'

'Possible.'

'And you weren't going to tell me?'

He shrugged. 'Ever since I lost my wife, it's been real hard for me to say goodbye to any woman.'

'I can understand that. But what I can't understand is why you want to say goodbye in the first place. We haven't known each other very long, but I got the impression that you had feelings for me.'

'I was attracted to you, if that's what you mean.'

'But not enough to keep you from riding on?'

'I reckon not.'

'Then to hell with you!' Lorna slammed the door in Coop's face.

He stood there, wondering if he'd made a mistake. Momentarily he wavered. Then in his mind he heard Gospel's voice telling him not to waste his bullets here; that there were clean sheets waiting elsewhere for him.

Knowing that Gospel was referring to Gabriela, Coop felt reassured and headed for the livery stable. Before reaching it, though, he stopped in at the telegraph office and on a hunch, checked the wire service between Rocas Rojas and El Paso to see if there had been any other recent train robberies.

The answer made him smile grimly.

23

It was still dark the next morning when Coop crossed over into Mexico. But as he rode parallel to the border, following the winding trail that Gospel had taken on their previous ride to Del Gardo's ranch, dawn finally broke.

Yawning, Coop pulled the brim of his Stetson lower in order to shield his eyes from the rising sun. Even so, he still had to squint as slowly the bright morning light spilled over his face. His stoic expression didn't change, but inwardly he felt uplifted. Though jaded by most things in life, he'd never grown tired of seeing a new day dawning. It meant that despite all odds, he was still alive and that was reason enough to rejoice.

Today was no different. As Coop guided the weary buckskin across the parched and seemingly endless desert, he watched as the sun inched above the distant mountains. It rose slowly, the pale golden orb growing bigger and brighter. And though it was too early for Coop to feel any warmth from it, there was no denying the magnificent effect the sun had on the nude gray sky. He watched appreciatively as its rays flooded the heavens with pale green, pink and primrose streaks.

But the sunrise had another effect on Coop: it made him feel more alone than usual. That was because sunrises reminded him of Helen. She had always loved sunrises. Every morning before feeding the chickens, she stood at the gate of their tiny farm, elbows resting on the top bar, watching the sun rise above the far-off hills.

Now, as Coop closed his eyes and visualized his dead wife, he remembered how much happiness and contentment she had brought to his solitary life. But his joy only lasted for a few months. Then Fate had cruelly snatched Helen from him, leaving him alone once more.

Only now it was worse. Now he had someone to miss, to long for. Devastated by her death, the only way he could cope with being alone was by drinking himself into a stupor. And though eventually he'd sold the farm and willed himself to become sober, he'd never lost his craving for whiskey.

Just like now, he thought. Sweet Jesus, what he wouldn't do for a bottle of Red Eye. As he rode on, silently cursing himself for letting whiskey enter his thoughts, he knew he wouldn't be satisfied until he'd had a drink. Or maybe two or three . . .

24

It was full-on morning when Coop approached the far end of the valley that Gospel had called the Garden of Eden. The blue sky was still cloudless, allowing the sun to blaze down unimpeded, and both man and horse were sweating in the intense heat.

Thirsty, Coop reined up, dismounted and untied his kerchief from around his neck. He then uncapped his canteen and took a swig of the warm brackish water. It didn't quench his thirst — only whiskey could do that — but it helped. About to recap his canteen, he noticed the buckskin was slathered in sweat, and knowing they still had a ways to go he soaked his kerchief and squeezed out the water between the horse's lips.

The buckskin repaid Coop's kindness by trying to bite him. Coop jerked his hand away just in time and cursed the horse. The buckskin, as if knowing this was an on-going clash of wills, snorted, unperturbed, and turned away.

'Keep it up,' Coop warned, 'and I swear I'll sell you for dog meat — ' He broke off as he noticed smoke rising from behind the hills that hid his view of Don Del Gardo's *ranchero*. Even more alarmed was the amount of black smoke that was billowing upward. It was far more than any fireplace could produce and Coop suddenly realized that all that smoke could only mean one thing: the *hacienda* was on fire!

Fearing the worst, he swung up into the saddle and spurred the startled buckskin into a gallop. The hills were still two miles away and the ranch another half-mile beyond that, and as the horse pounded onward, past several large rock-strewn mounds, Coop tried to block out the grisly image that dogged his mind: Gabriella trapped in her bedroom by a wall of flames.

Praying that the image was wrong,

Coop whipped more speed out of the buckskin. Though already black with sweat the laboring horse bravely responded and soon the mounds of rocks fell behind them. Still, Coop didn't let up. He continued to whip the buckskin with the reins, and shortly they raced past the last of the rocky outcrops.

Now only the hills stood between himself and Del Gardo's ranch. But as Coop rode toward them, the billowing smoke became so dense it blacked out the sky. Even more alarming, he could hear sporadic gunfire mingled with women screaming and men raucously laughing and shouting in Spanish.

Realizing that *bandidos* must be attacking the *ranchero*, Coop tried not to picture how they would treat Gabriela. But it was impossible! The images kept forming and Coop, sickened by his thoughts, tried to whip more speed out of the faltering buckskin.

As he neared the hills, he heard horses approaching. Though he couldn't see who was riding them, he guessed it was the bandits returning to their hideout. He could tell there were too many of them for him to fight single-handedly, so he wheeled his horse around and raced back to the nearest rocky mound. On reaching it, he rode behind the rocks, dismounted, and levered a round into his carbine. Then resting it on top of a rock, he waited for the bandits to appear.

Soon, about thirty heavily-armed Mexican raiders came riding around the hill closest to Coop. Believing they wouldn't be pursued, they rode leisurely, the dust kicked up by their horses swirling around them so that they resembled ghost riders.

But ghosts they were not!

Coop only needed one look at their high-crowned sombreros, twin *bandoleros* crossed over their shoulders and saddles glinting with silver *conchos* to recognize them. It was equally obvious that they had just raided Del Gardo's ranch, for many of them held squawking chickens or squealing piglets, while the rest drank greedily from upturned kegs, the wine spilling from their mouths onto their shabby clothing.

As they rode toward Coop, he steeled himself for what would probably be his last fight. But luck was with him. The drunken bandits didn't see him. Led by Heraclio Bernal, whose face Coop recognized from wanted posters, they rode past the rocky mound toward their hideout in the hills of Northern Sinaloa. Driven along behind them was a herd of bellowing cattle. The steers passed so close to the rocky mound, Coop could see the letters EDG branded on their flanks. Recognizing the brand as Del Gardo's, his fear for Gabriela's safety increased tenfold.

Desperate to know if she was still alive, he forced himself to wait until the last of the bandits and the stampeding cattle had passed. He then sprang into the saddle and spurred the buckskin in the direction of the burning *hacienda*.

25

When Coop finally reined up at the entrance to Del Gardo's home, his worst fears became a reality. The front gates had been torn from their hinges and lay broken on the ground. Ahead, flames ravaged the blackened remains of the house, barn and bunkhouse. Everywhere, Del Gardo's men were desperately trying to put out the fires.

Coop rode up the driveway, jumped from his horse and quickly joined the line of ranch-hands and field workers frantically throwing buckets of water onto the flames. As he pitched in, he looked around for Gabriela and her father. Unable to see them in all the smoke, he asked one of the men if he knew where the Don was. The man thumbed at the well behind them. Coop hurried over to it and found Del Gardo helping his men to refill the empty buckets. The Don's face was bruised and swollen from the bandits' punches and his soiled clothing was spattered with his own blood.

'*Muy bandidos!*' he shouted before Coop could say anything. '*Estos hijos de los demonios*, they . . . they attack us without warning!'

'Yeah, they rode past me,' said Coop, adding: 'Where's Gabriela, *senor*? Is she safe?'

Del Gardo shook his head and sagged in despair.

'What is it? What's wrong?' Coop exclaimed when Del Gardo didn't answer. 'Tell me, *senor*! Where is she? What's happened to her?'

'She is . . . was . . . *secuestrado!*'

Coop's heart almost stopped. 'Kidnapped?' he repeated numbly.

'*Si, si, mi amigo* — ' Del Gardo broke down, sobbing.

Coop thought back, trying to picture the bandits as they rode past him. But though he could visualize them clearly in his mind, he couldn't recall seeing

Gabriela or any other prisoners riding among them. Then he remembered how much dust was swirling around the bandits and wondered if this was why he hadn't seen her.

'You sure about this?' he pressured Del Gardo. 'You couldn't be mistaken?'

'No, *senor*, I saw — '

'I mean, maybe Gabriela is . . . hiding somewhere . . . you know . . . where she can't be found and . . . is just waiting there until she's certain the bandits are not coming back?'

'No, no,' Del Gardo cried. 'I am not mistaken, *hombre*. With these two eyes, I see it happen . . . see these miserable sons of whores drag my precious Gabriela from the house and throw her over a horse . . . ' He stopped, too distraught to continue.

Coop gripped Del Gardo by the shoulders and forced the Don to look at him.

'Listen to me, *senor*!'

Del Gardo fought back his tears and looked up at the tall gunfighter.

'It's too late to save your house,' Coop said, 'but not Gabriela. If you'll let me take some of your men, I'll go after her and bring her back, no matter what it takes!'

'*Si, si*, take them!' Del Gardo exclaimed. 'Take them all! But please, please, *mi amigo*, bring my dear Gabriela back to me!'

'Got my word on it,' Coop promised grimly. 'Now, if you will, *senor*, order your men to arm themselves and get saddled up, *muy pronto*!'

26

Most of the men employed by Del Gardo were either local villagers or migrant field hands, known as *campesinos*. They were simple men. They worked hard when employed, but were equally happy when unemployed, choosing to sit around drinking tequila or beer while their women took care of the children and daily chores. None of them had any military training, but all could shoot a gun and were undisciplined when it came to organized fighting. But once aroused, they were fearless and Del Gardo had no trouble convincing them to ride with Coop in pursuit of the *bandidos*.

Saddling up, they gathered around the tall gunfighter in front of the burned ruins, brandishing antiquated rifles, pistols and machetes and vowing vengeance! Their excited shouting made the normally calm buckskin jittery and Coop ordered them to quiet down. Some of them obeyed, but most didn't. They were too fired up to listen to him and were still shouting death to the bandits when Coop led them into the desert.

The *bandidos'* trail was easy to follow. Confident that no one would dare pursue them, they had made no effort to cover their tracks or the tracks of the stolen cattle, and Coop and the *campesinos* were able to see them from horseback.

Even so, the *bandidos* had gotten a big head start and Coop, knowing their hideout was located in the hills of Northern Sinaloa, hoped he could overtake them long before then. He also knew that catching the bandits too soon had its risks. They not only outnumbered his force, but many of them were former soldiers who were accustomed to fighting under adverse conditions — something the *campesinos* weren't. They were also better armed, and Coop knew that to attack them in broad daylight would be suicidal for the unruly *campesinos* . . . and possibly for Gabriela, too.

No, he thought, their best chance to defeat the *bandidos* would be to wait until nightfall before overtaking them. By then most of the bandits would be drunk, making them vulnerable to a surprise attack; and while they were desperately trying to defend themselves in the dark, Coop hoped that in their drunken stupor they wouldn't be able to guard Gabriela, giving him a chance to rescue her.

But darkness was a double-edged sword. If for some reason the bandits decided to change directions or not return to their hideout, Coop knew darkness would make it more difficult to follow their tracks — *and* more dangerous. Worse, if the *campesinos* accidentally blundered into the bandits' camp, they'd be as surprised as the *bandidos*, thus evening the odds. And an even fight was the last thing Coop wanted.

Deciding not to leave anything to chance, he waited until they were in a sheltered *arroyo* and then reined up, bringing everyone to a halt. Gathering the *campesinos* around him, he told his tracker, a quiet, fierce-eyed young Apache named Joaquin Bonito, to ride on ahead and find the bandits' camp and where their lookouts were located and then report back to him. 'But be real careful,' he warned. 'Because if those bastards catch you, they'll kill you for sure — and believe me, they'll take their damn' sweet time doing it!'

'This I know,' Joaquin said calmly. 'But there is no need for worry, *El Jefe*. I will be quiet as smoke.'

27

When dusk eventually fell, the bandits made camp in a narrow, high-walled canyon that was full of rock piles. According to an ancient legend, huge amounts of gold had been found here, lending credence to its original name: *Barranca de Oro*.

Over the years the promise of gold had lured countless prospectors to the canyon. But despite all their digging on the rocky hillsides or panning in the creek that snaked through the canyon, none of them had ever found any ore or gold dust in their pans . . . and over time they became known as the Hard Luck Miners and the canyon was renamed *Suerto Canyon Duro*.

By now, as Coop had predicted, most of the *bandidos* were so drunk they couldn't walk and collapsed as soon as they dismounted. The few men who didn't pass out drunkenly staggered around until they found a place to sleep among the rocks.

Meanwhile, their leader, Heraclio, and his two lieutenants, Jesus Torres and Pablo Ramirez sat on a low rise overlooking the stolen cattle below. They shared a bottle of *tequila*, but were still sober as they haggled over the amount of Gabriela's ransom.

Behind them was the mouth of a small cave that was protected on three sides by massive boulders. Armed lookouts kept watch on top of the boulders, while below at the campfire two tough female bandits with dark fierce eyes, unkempt black hair and pistols tucked in their belts, spit-roasted a calf carcass for the evening meal.

Gabriela sat huddled just inside the cave, listening to Heraclio and his lieutenants arguing over her ransom. She was bound and gagged, her hair was a tangled mess, her clothes torn and dirty ... her face bruised and swollen by the bandit leader's blows.

She was also frightened, but stubbornly refused to show it. Earlier she had tried to convince Heraclio to let her go, promising that her father would pay any ransom the bandits demanded. On the other hand, she warned, if he didn't release her, he and his men would be hunted by not only the *Rurales* and *Federales* but also every bounty hunter on both sides of the border, all eager to claim the reward offered by her father.

It was the wrong thing to say. Heraclio, contemptuous of all women, especially *gringo* women, became angered by Gabriela's 'imperious tone,' and responded by beating her bloody. He then tied her up, gagged her and warned her that if she made a sound or tried to escape, he'd shoot her.

Gabriela knew he meant it. She spoke enough Spanish to eavesdrop and soon after being kidnapped, she'd heard Heraclio telling his lieutenants that if her father tried to stall the negotiations or delayed paying the ransom in order to give the soldiers more time to capture them, they should kill Gabriela so that she didn't hinder their escape. In fact, he added, as the idea appealed to him, maybe it would be safer to kill her anyway. Then they wouldn't have to worry about keeping her prisoner.

Jesus and Pablo protested, claiming that once Gabriela was dead they'd lose the ransom. Heraclio laughed contemptuously and called them *estupido*! They could still get the ransom, no matter whether she was alive or dead. All they had to do was insist that her father pay them first before revealing where his daughter was and then hole up in their hideout until the authorities stopped looking for them!

His lieutenants weren't convinced. They might get away with it, they argued. But once people heard they had killed their hostage, from then on if they kidnapped someone else nobody would pay them ransom money again.

As Gabriela listened to the bandits arguing, she realized her only hope of surviving was either by escaping or if

Coop or her father rescued her before Heraclio bullied his followers into killing her. It was a frightening thought, especially since she knew there was little chance of her being rescued. And though she was no coward, the fact that death seemed inevitable scared her and she couldn't stop trembling.

28

It was dark and bitterly cold in the *arroyo*. Coop sat by the tethered buckskin, hat pulled over his eyes, back against his saddle, blanket draped about his shoulders, his gloved hands massaging his legs in an effort to chase the numbness from his feet.

All around him, the restless *campesinos* sat huddled under their *serapes*. Though their sombreros hid their faces, Coop could hear them grumbling among themselves. He couldn't hear everything they said, but he heard enough to realize they were angry at him for not letting them pursue the bandits. And as their grumbling grew more persistent, he knew he couldn't keep them here much longer against their will.

Dammit, he thought, where the hell was Joaquin Bonito? Pushing aside his blanket, he pulled out his pocket watch, flared a match on his thumbnail and checked the time. It had been almost an hour since the young tracker had left. Wondering how much longer the Apache would be, Coop started to return the watch to his pocket. But, as always, he felt compelled to look fondly at it for a moment.

It was an old, much-dented timepiece made by the now-defunct Lancaster Watch Company. It didn't keep time accurately, losing a minute daily, but it had belonged to his pa and that made it special. It was the only link Coop had to his deceased father, a soldier who had survived the Civil War only to be gunned down a few years later by a bounty hunter who mistook him for an outlaw, and momentarily Coop felt a lump forming in his throat. Not wanting to deal with the pain he knew would follow, he quickly fought down his emotions, returned the watch to his pouch and reached for his tobacco pouch. As he did, angry voices erupted in front of him. He looked at the *campesinos* and saw that two of them were on their feet, arguing over the fact that the younger man had insulted the older man's sister. Both men were furious and finally, egged on by the other *campesinos*, they started fighting.

Throwing off his blanket, Coop jumped up, yelling: '*Basta*! *Basta*!'

They ignored him and continued fighting. Coop moved closer and kicked their feet out from under them. Startled, both men thumped to the ground. The fall knocked the wind from them and for a few moments they sat there, trying to catch their breath.

Coop pulled out Gospel's knife, grabbed the nearest fighter and pressed the blade against his throat. 'Listen up,' he told the *campesinos*, 'because I'm only going to say this once . . . ' He paused to make sure he had their attention before continuing. 'The next one of you makes any trouble, I'll slit this fella's throat! *Comprende*?'

The *campesinos* stared silently at

him, their expressions hard to read.

'*Comprende?*'

The *campesinos* grudgingly nodded.

'*Bueno!*' Coop returned Gospel's knife to its sheath as if the matter was settled. But he knew by their sullen faces that despite obeying him, they were so worked up and eager to rescue Gabriela that unless Joaquin returned soon, he'd have a mutiny on his hands. He had already angered them earlier by refusing to let them build a fire. It was too risky, he explained. If the bandits saw the fire, they'd know someone was after them and in their hurry to escape, might kill Gabriela rather than turn her free. 'Is that what you want?' Coop demanded. 'The *señorita's* death on your conscience?'

The *campesinos* grudgingly shook their heads.

'Fair enough,' Coop said. 'Then all of you, go sit down! You heard me! *Vete a sentarte!*'

The *campesinos* obeyed, and returned to where they had been sitting.

Satisfied, Coop returned to the buckskin, sat down and leaned back against his saddle. A bitter wind had sprung up, making it bone-chillingly cold, and he quickly wrapped the blanket about him. He then removed his gloves, got out his tobacco pouch and tried to build a smoke. But despite the gloves, his fingers were numb and after two fumbling attempts and a lot of spilled tobacco, Coop returned the makings to his pocket and sat there, shivering under the blanket, awaiting Joaquin's return.

Fortunately, the same cold wind chased clouds across the moon. As a result there was very little moonlight and Coop, as he sat yearning for a smoke, blessed the darkness, knowing it would hide Joaquin as he searched for the bandits' camp.

Thinking of the bandits reminded Coop of Gabriela, and he prayed that she hadn't been tortured or raped by her ruthless captors. It was an ugly thought and he tried to block it from his mind. But it was impossible. The idea of Gabriela being in their hands filled him with a sense of helplessness that was so frustrating, all he wanted to do was kill someone — *anyone*!

And at times when he managed to stop thinking of Gabriela, his craving for whiskey returned and gave him the shakes. As he angrily cursed himself, he heard a horse approaching and got to his feet. The *campesinos* also heard the horse's hooves and jumping up, they eagerly awaited the in-coming rider.

Moments later, Joaquin Bonito rode out of the darkness. Reining up his lathered horse, he dismounted and tucked his Springfield Model 1873 trapdoor rifle into its scabbard. Then pushing aside his excited comrades, he proudly confronted Coop.

'I do all you ask of me, *El Jefe*!'

'Meaning you found them — the *bandidos*!'

'*Si, Senor* Coop. I find them. I find where they sleep. I find where their lookouts sit. Where their fires burn. And

I count how many *hombres* who are — are — '

'*Borracho?*'

'*Si, si, muy borracho!*'

'*Bueno!*' exclaimed Coop. 'If the bastards are drunk, they can't fight us.'

'This is true, *Jefe*. They no can fight. No can hold gun. Too much *tequila!*'

'What about Gabriela? Did you see her?'

'No, *Jefe*. But I see cave near fire. It is in here I believe she is held prisoner.'

'Makes sense,' Coop agreed. 'And the bandits' camp — how far is it?'

'Only two hills in distance.'

'And you can lead us there?'

'*Si, si,* I lead. Not far. I lead you easy.'

'Great!' Coop said, clapping Joaquin on the back. 'Good work, *amigo!*'

'*Gracias, El Jefe.*'

'Okay, you heard him,' Coop told the *campesinos*. 'Saddle up! Get moving! *Montarse! Montarse!*'

29

With Joaquin Bonito leading the way, Coop and the *campesinos* rode through the dark hills until the young Apache raised his hand, indicating they were close to the bandits' camp. Coop and the *campesinos* reined up, dismounted and tied their horses to the clumps of mesquite growing profusely alongside the trail.

'How much farther, *amigo?*' Coop asked Joaquin.

The young Apache pointed some fifty yards ahead, where a narrow sandy gully cut between two low scrub-covered hills and disappeared into the darkness beyond.

'Just on other side of hills, *El Jefe*.'

'And you're sure this is where the bandits are holed up?'

'*Si, si*. They sleep among many big rocks.'

'What about lookouts?'

'I find them, too. They sit there and there,' Joaquin indicated places on both hills. 'They are hidden behind much brush, faces turned toward us.'

'So, how do we sneak past them?'

'We not sneak past, *Jefe*. We wait till clouds swallow moon. Then I show you where they hide and we — ' He drew his hand, knifelike, across his throat.

'Fair enough,' Coop said. He turned to the eagerly awaiting *campesinos*. 'Wait here, *hombres*. We'll be right back!'

Resentful about being left behind, the *campesinos* immediately started protesting.

Joaquin quickly gestured for them to be quiet. '*Silencio, amigos! Silencio!* You must obey *Senor* Coop! If you do not, *Senorita* Gabriela, she will die!'

Reluctantly, the *campesinos* simmered down.

'I hope they ain't going to be a problem,' Coop said as he followed Joaquin up the nearest hill. 'We already got more trouble than we can handle.'

'No problem,' Joaquin assured. 'I know these *hombres*. They listen to me. I give my word.'

'No offense, *compadre*, but your word might mean something to me, but to that bunch of cabbage pickers, hell, it ain't worth a bent nickel!'

'Please, *Jefe*, do not be angry with them. I tell you true. These *hombres*, they not mean to defy you. They no understand your ways. Much patience is needed, for they are like little *ninos*.'

'Some children,' Coop growled.

The lookout sat halfway up the steep rocky hillside, facing the gully. A hardened veteran with a battle-scarred brown face and missing teeth, he gripped an old bolt-action rifle and cocked his head as he listened for any suspicious noises. Hidden by brush, he was barely visible even when the moon was out; when it was hidden by drifting clouds, he couldn't be seen by anyone approaching from the gully.

Coop, once Joaquin pointed him out,

couldn't help but admire the tracker's ability to spot the lookout. But knowing praise might embarrass him, as it did most Apaches, Coop kept silent and together the two men cautiously worked their way up the hillside.

Physically, it was an easy climb. But what wasn't easy was scrambling up the slope without disturbing the ground underfoot. Knowing that the sound of dirt and stones slithering down the hill would alert the lookout that someone was approaching, Coop and Joaquin took their time. Occasionally, they paused and listened, craning their necks as they peered up through the darkness to see if the bandit was looking their way. When they were sure he wasn't, they slowly continued climbing toward him.

Luck was with them. The moon remained hidden by drifting clouds for almost the entire time it took them to ascend the slope and duck behind the rocks just below the brush hiding the lookout. There, they paused to catch their breath. Then Coop mimed that he wanted Joaquin to work his way around in front of the lookout and deliberately make a noise to attract his attention. 'While he's looking your way,' Coop whispered, 'I'll jump him from behind and make sure he don't yell out.'

Joaquin nodded to show he understood and crawled off into the darkness.

Coop reached back, under his shirt, and drew Gospel's knife. He then inched closer to the ring of brush. When he was within a few feet, he heard the lookout stir. Coop froze, and moments later saw the lookout stand up and stretch the stiffness from his arms and legs.

His back was to Coop, who was tempted to jump him. But knowing that Joaquin wasn't in position yet and might be exposed to a stray bullet if the lookout got off a shot, Coop restrained himself and remained still.

Shortly, he heard Joaquin's signal: the sound of dirt and stones slithering down the slope on the other side of the hill.

Instantly, the lookout aimed his rifle in the direction of the noise.

Before he could fire, Coop hurled himself over the brush. He struck the lookout from behind, knocking him down and sending his rifle flying. Coop then quickly straddled the husky bandit, pinning him to the ground. As the lookout struggled to break loose, Coop jerked the man's head back and slashed his throat. The lookout gagged as he choked on his own blood and went limp. Coop waited a moment, knife raised, ready to stab the bandit again should he move. But the man was dead.

Tucking the knife away, Coop got to his feet and saw Joaquin peering over the brush at him. 'One down, *compadre*,' he whispered.

Joaquin nodded impassively and motioned for Coop to follow him. Together, they quietly descended the slope, moving carefully so as not to disturb any dirt or stones, and didn't stop until they reached the bottom of the hill.

'You say this yahoo's about halfway

up?' Coop said, eyeing the other steep hillside.

'*Si, si*. Maybe little higher.'

'*Perfecto!*' Coop wearily rolled his eyes.

'It would be my honor, *Jefe*, if you would permit me to kill him myself.'

Coop grinned ruefully. 'Thanks, *compadre*. But we started out together and that's how we'll finish. *Venga!*'

30

During their climb up the second hill the moon wasn't as cooperative. It kept appearing from behind the drifting clouds, each time its radiant silvery glow lighting up the night and, more importantly, the hillside.

'Damn,' Coop whispered as the moonlight continually forced them to duck behind the rocks. 'This keeps up, *compadre*, we'll be here till goddamn sunup!'

Joaquin didn't answer. Deep in thought, he suddenly turned to Coop and stretched one leg out to him. 'Untie, *Jefe*, *por favor*,' he whispered.

'What?'

'Lace, lace, untie!' Without waiting for Coop to respond, Joaquin started removing the thin leather thong that laced up his other knee-high moccasin.

Coop followed suit. 'What's your plan?' he asked softly.

'Wait. You see, *Jefe*.'

Coop said no more. Quickly unthreading the lace, he handed it to Joaquin. The Apache grabbed it and tied it around a small rock he'd found. He then tied his lace around another, similar-sized rock and knotted both thongs together. Motioning for Coop to stay still, he patiently waited until the drifting clouds once more covered the moon and then quietly climbed the remaining distance to the brush hiding the lookout.

Coop, straining to see in the darkness, watched Joaquin's every move. At the same time he kept his hand near his revolver, ready to draw if the Apache needed help.

Once Joaquin was close to the lookout, he stopped, got to his knees and began twirling the rocks around above his head. As he did, he hooted, owl-like, the sound inducing the lookout to peer over the brush in Joaquin's direction.

Immediately, the Apache hurled the twirling rocks at him. The alarmed lookout raised his rifle, ready to shoot.

But he was too late. Like a bolas, the rocks and thongs wrapped around his neck, choking off any sound he tried to make.

Unable to breathe, the lookout dropped his rifle and desperately tried to loosen the strangling leather thongs. But before he could, Joaquin was on him, stabbing him repeatedly in the chest.

'*Numero dos*,' he said as Coop joined him.

Coop sighed gratefully. 'Let's hope that's all of them, *compadre*. These here boots of mine, they ain't made for climbing hills.'

'*Grunidos, grunidos, grunidos!*'

Coop chuckled. 'You'd grumble too, you damned heathen, if you had my blisters!'

Joaquin laughed softly. 'Maybe I should carry you down the hill, *Jefe*.'

'That'll be the day,' Coop growled. Turning, he slowly made his way down the hillside. Joaquin followed. Both men moved carefully, each trying not to kick any stones or dirt loose. It hampered their progress, forcing them to move slower than they wished, and by the time they finally reached the bottom of the hill their patience was pushed to the limit.

Without pausing to catch their breath, the two of them hurried back to the *arroyo*. The drifting clouds chose this moment to cover the moon, making it difficult to see in the darkness. But Joaquin seemed to have the eyes of a cat and unerringly led the way through the dense brush and rocks. Coop stumbled along behind him, trying to be as quiet as possible.

As they entered the *arroyo*, the impatient *campesinos* swarmed around them, brandishing their rifles and machetes, demanding to know if Coop or Joaquin had found the bandit camp and seen Gabriela.

Coop held up his hand for silence. 'There ain't time to explain,' he told them. 'If we want to save Gabriela's life, we've got to hurry. *Pronto! Pronto!*' He turned back to Joaquin, waited for the Apache to take the lead and then signaled to the *campesinos* to follow them.

31

Once beyond the two low hills, they filed quietly through the narrow gully and soon reached the slope where the *bandidos* were sleeping among the rocks. They could also see the leaders dozing by the fire and, behind them, the entrance to the cave.

Coop moved close to Joaquin and whispered: 'It's important for the men to know they got to cut each bandit's throat. Because if one of them cries out or gets a shot off before they kill him, it could be curtains for Gabriela.'

'Do not worry,' Joaquin assured. 'I make sure they understand this clearly.'

'Thanks,' Coop said. 'But I think it's better if they hear it from me.'

'As you wish, *Jefe*.'

Coop faced the *campesinos* and carefully choosing his words, said grimly: '*Es muy importante que cortar las gargantas de estos hombres para que no gritar! Entender?'*

The *campesinos* nodded with equal grimness.

'*Si incluso un hombre grita, Gabriela puede morir!*'

Again, the men before him nodded.

Satisfied, Coop looked up and saw that the clouds were about to cover the moon. He signaled to the *campesinos* to spread out and wait for his signal before moving in. The *campesinos* drew their machetes and took up their positions, all eyes on Coop.

He waited until the first of the clouds drifted over the moon and then signaled to the *campesinos*. They obeyed, moving swiftly and silently to the sleeping bandits, and within moments the slaughter began.

Coop and Joaquin picked out their victims and crept up to them. The two *bandidos* had passed out by the rocks facing the campfire. The fire was almost out, but the dying embers gave off enough light for Coop to see Heraclio and his lieutenants dozing near a small cave. It was too dark to see inside the cave, but Coop hoped this was where Gabriela was being held prisoner.

A sudden drunken snore from one of the bandits interrupted Coop's thoughts. Drawing his knife, he pressed his hand over the unconscious bandit's mouth and cut the man's throat. The bandit went limp. Coop glanced over at Joaquin. The young Apache was kneeled beside a dead bandit, wiping the blood from his knife blade.

Coop pointed at the cave and signaled to Joaquin to follow him. Joaquin obeyed and together, they crawled between the scattered rocks, on up the slope toward the cave. As they neared Heraclio and his two lieutenants, the bandit leader stirred, yawned, and seemed about to wake up.

Coop and Joaquin froze. But it was a false alarm. After a little Heraclio settled back down and didn't stir again. Coop and Joaquin eased past the bandit leader and crept to the cave entrance.

They peered inside. It was still too dark for them to see anyone, but they could hear movement in the cave.

Coop took a match from his shirt pocket and struck it on his thumbnail. Then shielding the flame with his free hand, he peered into the cave and saw Gabriela huddled against one wall. For a moment she stared fearfully at him; then, relief quickly replaced her fear as she recognized Coop. He held his finger against his lips, warning her not to make a sound. She nodded to show she understood and indicated her wrists and ankles so he could see she was tied up.

Coop motioned for Joaquin to keep watch and crawled into the cave. As he reached Gabriela, the match went out. Coop lit another match, wedged it in a crack in the rock wall and quickly cut her free. Gabriela closed her eyes, briefly overcome with relief. She then smiled gratefully at Coop and began rubbing her numbed wrists and ankles to get the blood circulating.

The match flame fluttered, ready to die out. Coop quickly lit his last match, held it in front of his face and mouthed something to Gabriela. She frowned and shook her head, unable to understand him.

He leaned close and whispered: 'Don't move. Be right back.'

32

Once outside the cave, Coop rejoined
Joaquin. The young Apache already had
his knife out, eager to stab the nearest
bandit. Coop motioned for him to put
the knife away, drew his Dance
Brothers .44 and mimed striking the
bandits on the head. Disappointed,
Joaquin grudgingly sheathed his knife
and picked up a fist-sized rock. Then,
side-by-side, he and Coop crawled up
behind the three bandits.

Coop raised his revolver but didn't
strike Heraclio until Joaquin was in
position behind Pablo Ramirez. Then,
in unison, they each clubbed their
victims. Both bandits slumped, unconscious, to the ground.

Coop quickly moved to Jesus Torres,
who was snoring in his sleep. Coop
struck him on the head, knocking him
senseless. He then looked back at

Gabriela, who was peering out of the cave, and beckoned to her. As she crawled to him, the moon slid from behind the clouds. Coop turned to Joaquin and whispered: 'Find something to tie these bastards up with. Come sunup, we're taking them with us. I want to see them swing for kidnapping Gabriela — ' He broke off as gunfire erupted below them.

They looked down the slope and at the bottom, saw a dozen groggy-looking bandits firing at the *campesinos*. The field hands, having left their antiquated firearms with their horses, were unarmed save for their bloodstained machetes, but they still bravely attacked the bandits.

This time, the bandits stood their ground and relentlessly gunned down the charging *campesinos*. Their gunfire aroused other bandits who were still alive. They staggered up and opened fire at the onrushing field hands. Many of the *campesinos* were cut down, while the rest quickly took cover.

At the top of the slope, Coop drew

his .44 and picked off several of the bandits. Joaquin, who'd left his rifle behind, ran to Pablo Ramirez, grabbed the unconscious bandit's pistol, rejoined Coop and started shooting at the bandits.

The bandits whirled around and returned fire.

The slew of bullets chased Coop and Joaquin behind the rocks. Coop, not liking the odds, told Joaquin to keep firing. He then crawled to Heraclio and dragged the still-unconscious bandit to his feet. Using him as a shield, Coop drew Gospel's knife and pressed the blade against Heraclio's throat. 'Tell those bastards to throw down their weapons,' he told Joaquin, 'or I'll cut out the sonofabitch's Adam's Apple!'

Joaquin obeyed.

The bandits stopped firing and stood there, not sure what to do.

'Reckon they need persuading,' Coop said grimly. He cut the skin under Heraclio's Adam's Apple, drawing blood.

The bandits got Coop's message and grudgingly dropped their weapons.

33

Once the bandits had surrendered Coop released Heraclio, who slumped limply to the ground beside Pablo and Jesus. Coop then gave his carbine to Gabriela and told her to keep the prisoners covered.

'What if they try to escape?' she asked.

'Shoot them!'

'I hope it doesn't come to that,' she said. 'I want to turn them over to the marshal and see them legally hanged.'

'Before that can happen,' Coop reminded, 'we got to get them to town!' He turned back to the unarmed bandits, standing before him. Ordering them to lay down on the dirt, he warned them that he'd kill the first man who moved. Next he told Joaquin to drive off the bandits' horses. 'Make sure you scatter them broncs good, *compadre*. I don't want those chili-eaters bushwhacking us before we get to the ranch.'

'Do not worry, *Jefe*,' Joaquin assured. 'It will be as you ask. I will also make sure that their guns cannot shoot.'

'Fair enough,' Coop said. 'And tell the *campesinos* to round up the stolen cattle.'

'*Si, Jefe* . . . ' Joaquin hurried off.

Coop turned to Gabriela, who was still covering the prisoners. 'I'll handle them from here,' he said. He forced the three bandits to get on their knees and roped their hands behind their backs.

'You're not going to shoot them, are you?' Gabriela said, concerned.

'I'd like to,' Coop replied grimly. 'But that would be cheating your pa.' Before she could question what he meant, he added: 'You strong enough to walk a ways?'

'Yes.'

'Good. It ain't far to the horses. But if you get tired, tell me and I'll carry you.' He uncoiled his lariat and looped it over the three prisoners. Jerking the noose tight, he roped them together so that when one moved, they all had to move. He next signaled to Joaquin and the *campesinos* to start moving the cattle. Then, with Gabriela beside him, he started for the sheltered arroyo where they'd left their horses.

*   *   *

Upon reaching the arroyo, Coop instructed the *campesinos* to drive the cattle back to Del Gardo's spread, while he, Joaquin and *Senorita* Gabriela rode on ahead with the prisoners.

The *campesinos* didn't argue, but they exchanged uneasy looks. Joaquin, reading their expressions, suggested to Coop that he remain with the field hands.

'Why?' Coop asked. 'Do you reckon they'll make off with the beef?'

'No, no, *Jefe*. They not steal cattle. But this is work they not used to. Maybe they not watch them so good and lose many strays.'

'Fair enough,' Coop said. He turned to leave, then changed his mind and stuck out his hand to Joaquin. 'Look, if we don't meet up again, it's been aces riding with you.'

Joaquin grinned and shook hands. 'For me too, *Jefe. Hasta la vista!*'

'Same to you, *compadre.*' Coop gave a quick wave goodbye and rejoined Gabriela. He helped her to mount one of the saddled horses. Then untying the buckskin's reins, he stepped up into the saddle, looped the end of his lariat around the saddle horn and tapped the horse with his spurs. Though it was only a light tap, the irascible buckskin responded by trying to bite Coop's foot. But Coop was ready for him and jerked his boot from the stirrup.

'Quit that, dammit!' he cursed. 'Or I'll feed you to the wolves!'

The buckskin snorted, tossed its head in defiance and broke into a lazy trot. The lariat stretching from the saddle horn to the prisoners snapped taut, almost jerking Heraclio and the other two bandits off their feet. Recovering, they were forced to jog in order to keep up. Roped together as they were, it wasn't easy and shortly Pablo stumbled and fell . . . his weight pulling Heraclio and Jesus down with him.

Coop heard them yelling as they were dragged along, but ignored them.

Gabriela quickly reined up, begging: 'Stop, stop! Please, Coop, stop! These men, I know they are murderers. And I will gladly watch them hang for what they did to me and papa. But I cannot watch them being skinned alive.'

Coop reluctantly reined up. 'You got any idea what Heraclio had in store for you if you hadn't been rescued?' he asked her grimly.

'No,' Gabriela said. 'But I know it would not have been pleasant.'

'Pleasant?' Coop repeated sourly. 'Missy, I hate to muddy up those pure thoughts of yours, but after these gutless misfits had their fun with you, they would've given you to the men, so they could pleasure themselves and then — *then* after they got done, if you were still alive, they would've sold you to the Comanches. And I reckon I don't need to tell you how the young bucks would've treated you.'

'No, you don't,' Gabriela replied with a shudder. 'What's more, I know everything you say is true. Even my father has said as much. And not just to me, but to my sisters as well when he thought they were being too naïve. But, you see — and I don't expect you to understand this — much as I hate these men, I can't agree to torture them or I could never live with myself.'

'Fair enough,' Coop said. 'We'll leave them to the hangman's rope.'

As they slowly rode on, the truth hit Coop. Much as he cared for Gabriela, they had nothing in common. And knowing that, he sadly realized he was going to be a drifter for the rest of his life.

34

They rode on in silence. It was still dark and cold enough for their breath to show, but a sympathetic moon dodged the clouds and obligingly lighted their way. Alone, they could have made better time. But in order for the three bandits to keep up with them, they were forced to ride slowly and it was almost sunup when they finally reached Del Gardo's *rancho*.

The sight that greeted them devastated Gabriela. The once-magnificent house was nothing but smoldering, charred ruins. The nearby barn and bunkhouse had also been burned to the ground. Only the stables and storage sheds remained standing.

Dismounting, Coop helped Gabriela off her horse and stood back as an exhausted, smoke-blackened Del Gardo limped up to them. Behind him, the loyal ranch-hands who had stayed to help put out the fire continued to poke around in the ruins, looking for any still-glowing embers among the ashes.

Del Gardo tearfully hugged Gabriela with more emotion than he had ever displayed before. She joyfully responded and for several moments they remained embraced. The Don then gratefully thanked Coop for saving his daughter's life. 'It is impossible for me to find the words to thank you, *mi amigo*,' he said through his tears. 'But know that I am forever in your debt. And if there is ever anything you want, you have but to ask and it is yours!'

Coop sighed wearily. 'A nice soft bed and a bottle of *tequila* come to mind,' he said, eying the blackened ruins. 'But right now, I reckon they're a tad hard to get.'

'You are correct about the bed, *mi amigo*,' Del Gardo agreed, 'unless you do not mind sleeping in the stables. As for *tequila*,' he looked pointedly at his foreman, Javier Garza, 'this, I am sure we can oblige you with.'

Javier took the hint, '*Un momento, por favor*,' and hurried off to the grain shed. Entering it, he reappeared a few moments later, holding a small much-used keg and sheepishly brought it to Coop. 'Here, *senor*. *Disfruta!*'

'*Gracias, amigo*.'

'No, don't!' Gabriela exclaimed as Coop took the keg. 'That's *mezcal*!'

'That's okay,' Coop said, removing the plug. 'I like *mezcal*.'

'But this *mezcal*, it is different,' Gabriela warned. 'Javier, he make it himself with many other ingredients that make it much stronger.'

'Gabriela is right,' agreed her father. 'It would be wise to drink cautiously.' He watched as Coop prepared to take a drink, then said: 'Here in Mexico, we have a saying: *Mezcal* should not be downed, it should be kissed.'

'In other words, sip it,' Coop said. 'Sounds reasonable.' With everyone looking on, he tilted the keg to his lips and sipped. Then, immediately hooked by the alcohol, he took a long gulp. The homemade *mezcal* went down like molten lava sprinkled with chili peppers. Coop gasped and his eyes watered.

'I warned you,' Gabriela chided.

Coop ignored her. He raised the keg again and took another big gulp. This time he didn't grimace or gasp and his eyes didn't water. Instead, to everyone's amazement, he lowered the keg, grinned at them and said hoarsely: 'Just like I remembered: smooth as mother's milk.'

'If you will excuse my rudeness for speaking,' Javier said to Coop. 'It would seem, *senor*, you have drunk the *mezcal* before.'

'More times than I like to admit,' Coop replied. His eyes clouded with memories. 'You could say I grew up on it and — ' He broke off as if he'd inadvertently revealed an embarrassing secret; and then, before anyone could question him on it, he tucked the keg under one arm and thumbing at Heraclio, Pablo and Jesus, spoke to Del Gardo. 'These *hombres*, *senor*, they're the ones who burned you out and took Gabriela, here. Come sunup, maybe you'd like to watch them dancing from a rope.'

'*Si, si*, this would please me greatly!' Del Gardo said.

'No, papa,' Gabriela broke in. 'You cannot do this! Evil as these men are, if you lynch them, you will be no better than them.'

Her father ignored her. 'Lock them in the grain shed till the sun rises,' he told Javier. 'Then bring them to Hangman's Oak — ' He stopped abruptly as suddenly Heraclio managed to work his hands free and threw himself at Coop.

Coop went sprawling. Heraclio straddled him, pinning Coop to the ground, and grabbed for his six-shooter. Coop grasped the bandit leader's hand and hurled him aside. Both men sprang up and charged each other. They grappled fiercely and fell to the ground, rolling over and over, until finally Heraclio broke free and kicked the gun from Coop's hand. The .44 skidded across the dirt and stopped several feet away.

Heraclio dived for the six-shooter, grabbed it, whirled and went to shoot Coop.

But Coop had already reached behind his back, under his shirt, and in one fluid motion pulled Gospel's knife from its sheath and threw it at Heraclio.

The blade buried in the bandit leader's throat.

Heraclio staggered back, eyes saucers, gagging on his own blood. He dropped the gun and desperately grabbed for the knife. But death had already claimed him. And as his life flowed from the wound, he slumped to the ground . . . dead.

Coop limped to the corpse, pulled out Gospel's knife and wiped the blade clean on Heraclio's shirt. Justice is served, he thought grimly. Returning the knife to its sheath, he picked up his gun, thumbed the hammer back and faced the other bandits.

'No, no, don't!' Gabriela begged. 'Please, Coop. No more killing!'

'They burned our house and stole you from me,' her father said angrily. '*Madre de Dios*, child, surely you would not set them free?'

'Our house we can build again,' Gabriela said, 'and I am safely back with you, papa. That is all that matters ... ' She paused and looked at Coop, pleading: 'Please, do not start our life together with death. It will haunt us forever.'

Coop shrugged. 'Reckon it's up to you,' he said to Del Gardo.

'If it is my daughter's wish,' the ageing Don replied, 'so it shall be.' To Javier he added: '*Su machete, por favor.*'

Javier pulled his machete from his waistband and handed it to Del Gardo.

Del Gardo confronted Pablo and Jesus. Both looked fearfully at him.

'*Dame tu mano,*' he told Pablo.

The bandit hesitated. Then, trembling, he held out his right hand.

Del Gardo grasped Pablo's wrist and spread his fingers. Then with a swift, single stroke he cut off the bandit's forefinger. Pablo screamed and staggered back, nursing his bleeding hand.

Del Gardo turned to Jesus and gestured for him to hold out his hand. When Jesus refused, Javier grabbed his wrist and after a struggle forcibly held out his hand.

Del Gardo swung the machete, slicing off Jesus' forefinger.

Jesus gasped in pain and clutched his injured hand, trying to slow the bleeding.

'If I ever see either of you again,' Del Gardo warned the bandits, 'I will cut off more than a finger! Now, go!'

Pablo and Jesus stumbled away, trying to dodge the rocks that the jeering ranchhands hurled at them.

'It is done,' Del Gardo said, returning the machete to Javier. 'Now, as my daughter says, it is time to rebuild our lives!'

'Amen,' said Coop. Raising the keg of *mezcal*, he toasted the rising sun. 'To a new day! And to us,' he added to Gabriela, 'and the wonderful life we're going to share together.'

Gabriela smiled happily. Then noticing how shocked and displeased her father looked, she said: 'I know this is a surprise, papa. But I hope you will find it in your heart to give us your blessings.'

'You, my daughter,' Del Gardo replied gruffly, 'have always had my blessings. As for you,' he said resentfully to Coop, 'you have betrayed my trust!'

'I'm sorry you feel that way,' Coop said. 'I know this ain't how you folks normally do things down here, but you got to admit, *senor*, these ain't exactly normal times. I mean, between fighting off the bandits and getting your daughter back, there wasn't much time for courting.'

'So it would appear,' Del Gardo replied coldly.

'But come time for the wedding,' Coop continued, 'hopefully all that'll change and you and me, we'll see eye-to-eye on things.'

Del Gardo haughtily ignored Coop's

peace offering and spoke to his daughter. 'First, child, before we can talk about this foolishness, we must find somewhere to stay in town while the men build shelter for us here.'

'But Papa,' Gabriela began. 'I — '

'Hush, child,' her father chided. 'Once we are together, you and I, we have much to talk about.'

'But I want to be with Coop, papa. And he wants to be with me. Isn't that true?' Gabriela asked Coop.

'Sure,' he replied. 'But I still got to talk to your father.'

'No,' Gabriela said, flaring. 'This is between you and me, not papa!'

'Calm yourself, daughter,' Del Gardo soothed. 'If you will share this time with me, I propose a bargain — one you would be wise to consider.'

'Bargain?' Gabriela said, puzzled. 'What sort of bargain, papa?'

'If you agree not to marry this man, I will take you to your mother.'

For an instant Gabriela was so shocked, she couldn't respond. Then she gave her father a disgusted look and said: 'Shame on you, papa! Why do you lie to me? My mother, she is dead!'

'No, no, she is very much alive,' he corrected. 'And that is no lie, child . . . merely a truth she wished to hide from you.'

Stunned, Gabriela again couldn't find words to express herself.

Coop, uncomfortable to be a part of their quarreling, started to walk away.

'W-Where are you going?' Gabriela demanded.

Coop shrugged. 'Where I come from,' he said, 'family matters are private.' He was gone before she could stop him.

35

Gabriela watched sadly as Coop mounted his buckskin and rode off toward town. Though he hadn't said he wasn't returning, she sensed something terribly permanent about his departure and tears filled her lovely agate-green eyes. On top of her father's many lies, and the shock followed by the instant joy she'd felt on discovering her mother might be alive, the thought of losing Coop was more than she could take and she angrily turned to her father.

'See what you have done, papa?' she exclaimed. 'Thanks to you, I have lost the only man I ever loved. The man I wanted to be my husband.'

'That is foolish talk,' her father said. 'You are much too young to be considering marriage; especially to an older man who is nothing but a penniless drifter.'

'He may be a drifter,' Gabriela said scornfully, 'but at least he isn't a liar.'

'How dare you speak to me this way!'

'Lies,' Gabriela raged. 'Lies upon lies!'

'What lies?' demanded Del Gardo. 'What're you talking about?'

'I'm talking about the lie you just told me about my mother being alive, as well as all the other lies that you keep telling me in order to keep me here, with you, so you won't be left alone. That's it, isn't it, papa? You're afraid of being alone. It's a fear that has haunted you ever since mother died.'

Del Gardo seethed. He opened his mouth as if to chastise her, but no words came out. Frustrated, he turned his back to her, unable to deny her accusation.

Gabriela glared at his back and was about to continue her tirade, when she noticed that her father's shoulders were shaking. At the same time, she heard him sobbing. Immediately, her anger faded as quickly as it had come.

'Oh, papa,' she said, moving close to him, 'why must it always be this way between us? Surely by now you know that I love you . . . will always love you, no matter whether I am at your side or a thousand miles away.'

For a long moment Del Gardo didn't answer. Then he slowly turned and faced her. Tears streamed down his cheeks and his expression was full of shame and despair.

'Forgive me, child,' he begged. 'You're right, of course. I am afraid of being alone. I always have been. That's why the thought of you leaving fills me with dread and . . . '

'Anger?'

Her father sagged. 'Clearly, you have wisdom beyond your years, Gabriela. I have always known this and wrong as it is, I — '

'Hate me for it?'

'No, not hate, child. Never hate. But I do sometimes envy you for it. At the same time, I feel a loathing for myself that shames me to the core.'

'Oh, papa,' Gabriela said, fondly embracing him, 'you mustn't feel this way. You have nothing to be ashamed of — or to envy.'

'If only I could believe that,' her father said, fighting back his tears.

'Then believe this. Next time you're fearful or ashamed or . . . or envy me, remind yourself that without you I would not exist. Whatever I am, whatever good or bad is in me, is in you too. We are one and the same. Never forget that, papa.'

Del Gardo didn't say anything, but it was obvious he wasn't convinced.

'After all,' Gabriela continued, 'this wisdom you speak of, where do you think it came from?'

'Your dear departed mother, I suspect.'

Gabriela smiled tolerantly. 'Ah, yes, often I have heard you mention this to others. How everything wise and good in me came from my mother. But no one believes you, papa. Why should they? They know you much better than they knew my mother. And what they know about you demands respect.' She paused, expecting her father to say something. When he didn't, she added: 'As for myself, I was so young when mother passed away, I can barely remember her, let alone form an opinion — '

'Enough!' her father said suddenly. 'Let us speak no more of your mother's tragic death!'

'But — '

'*Silencio*, I say!' He grasped her arm, 'Come with me,' and despite her protests, led her to the stables.

Nor would he let her talk while they waited for one of the ranch-hands to harness a horse to the buckboard. The silence between them continued as they climbed aboard and Del Gardo drove in the direction of Rocas Rojas. But a mile or so before they reached the little town, he turned off onto a trail that led across the valley toward the hills.

'Please, papa,' Gabriela begged. 'Tell me where we are going.'

For several moments her father didn't answer. Then he grimly nodded to himself, knowing he'd just made an important decision, and said sternly: 'It is time you learned the truth about yourself, daughter.'

And that was all he would tell her.

36

Coop tied the buckskin up outside the Holy Moses, hitched up his gunbelt and entered the saloon. It was crowded with the usual drinkers and no one paid any attention to him as he made his way to the bar.

'Whiskey or tequila?' the tall bartender asked, recognizing him.

'Neither. I'm looking for Miss Lorna.'

'You'll have to get to the back of the line, mister. Seems like everybody's asking for her today.'

'So, where is she — upstairs or at home?'

'Neither,' the tall bartender said. 'She's out at her ranch.'

Coop, surprised that Lorna had never mentioned owning a ranch, said: 'And this ranch, friend, where might it be?'

'I ain't supposed to give that information out.'

'Fair enough,' Coop said. 'But be sure to tell Miss Lorna that when she has a snit fit because she didn't know I was riding on.'

The tall bartender shifted uncomfortably. 'When you put it like that, mister, reckon I'm dead either way, right?'

'Pretty much,' Coop admitted.

Sighing, the tall bartender made sure no one drinking at the bar could hear him, then leaned close to Coop and whispered the directions in his ear.

'You didn't hear that from me, remember?' he said, straightening up.

'Hear what?' Coop replied innocently.

The tall bartender grinned, winked at Coop and went back to work.

Coop elbowed his way through the crowd to the door. There, out of habit, he paused and looked back at the customers. Not recognizing anyone, friend or foe, he left the saloon, satisfied that he wasn't going to be followed and bushwhacked on the trail.

Lorna's ranch was an hour's ride out of town. Thanks to the tall bartender's directions, Coop found it easily. As he rode in through the open gate, he found himself confronted by a large well-kept ranch house, a barn and stables facing a bunkhouse. There were also several fenced corrals. All of them were empty save for the one nearest the house. It was occupied by a saddled, blue roan mare that Coop guessed belonged to Lorna. Otherwise the entire spread appeared to be deserted.

Slightly puzzled, Coop dismounted in front of the house and tied up the buckskin. As he climbed onto the porch, Lorna opened the door and stared at him in surprise.

'Coop!' she exclaimed. 'What the devil are you doing out here?'

'I wanted to say *adios*. I'm leaving town today and — '

'Permanently, you mean?'

'Uh-huh.'

'What about Gabriela?'

'What about her?'

'Oh, come now. Don't play dumb. This is a small town. Everyone knows everyone else's business. Why, you can't even sneeze without it being front-page news.'

'Fair enough,' Coop said. 'As far as I know, Gabriela's fine.'

'No wedding bells in sight?'

'None that are ringing for me.'

Lorna looked surprised. 'Does Miss Pure-of-heart know you're riding on?'

'She will.'

'In other words, you didn't tell her?'

'Saw no reason to.'

Lorna laughed sourly. 'I'd sure like to be there when she finds out.'

'Could always tell her yourself. See how she reacts.'

'I'm not *that* spiteful.'

'Reckon you'd only be disappointed anyway.'

'Meaning?'

'Could be, you're making this out to be a bigger molehill than it really is.'

'I hope so, for my sake. Or am I reading too much into this friendly visit?'

'Let's just say I'm here and leave it at that.'

'That suits me,' Lorna said. 'Now come on in, before you change your mind.'

Coop removed his hat and entered. He found himself in a large rustic room with a big stone fireplace and a beamed ceiling that served as a living room and bar.

'Brandy or whiskey?' Lorna asked, moving behind the bar.

'Reckon I'll pass,' Coop said, fighting down his craving.

'Really? Stop by the temperance union on your way in, did you?'

'Something like that,' Coop said wryly.

Lorna shrugged and poured herself a whiskey. 'As a matter of fact, I'm glad you dropped by. I'm leaving town myself soon and was hoping to see you before I left.'

'You sold the saloon, then?'

'Not yet. But I got two buyers from

back east. Both want it and I'm stalling in the hope of driving the price up.' She came around the bar and sat on the stool beside Coop. 'You know, cowboy, if you'd be willing to wait for a few days, maybe we could leave together.'

'And then what?'

'Then, nothing,' Lorna said. 'That's the fun of it. Treating every day like it's the last. Never boxing yourself in with promises you won't keep. That way, no one ever gets hurt.'

Coop had to admit there was a certain excitement to it. But not the kind of excitement he was looking for. 'Thanks. Reckon I'll keep drifting.'

Lorna looked disappointed. Then her smile returned, as did the sparkle in her eyes, and sipping her drink, she said: 'Suit yourself. But, know this: if we ever meet again, no matter when or where, the welcome mat is always out for you.'

'I'll keep that in mind,' Coop said, adding: 'There is one thing I'm curious about, though.'

'What?'

'Well, after seeing this spread and hearing you say you' re making money hand over fist, I can't figure out why the court wouldn't give you custody of your child.'

Lorna flinched as if he'd hit a nerve. 'Only the judge can answer that,' she said nervously. 'I mean, as we all know, things don't always have a happy ending.'

'Things?'

'Stuff we have no control over. And when that happens, you got a choice: you either let them destroy you or you try to get over them.'

'And you chose the latter?' Coop pressed.

Lorna didn't answer. She toyed briefly with her glass, watching the whiskey swirling around at the bottom, and then suddenly looked up at him.

'You were right,' she admitted. 'I lied.'

'About what?'

'My daughter. The courts actually awarded her to me, but I refused custody. I suppose I should be embarrassed to admit that, but I'm not, because it was the right thing to do.'

'How so?'

'I was unfit to be a mother.'

'Because you owned a saloon?'

'A saloon that's also a brothel. Jesus, I'm no saint, Coop, but I do have enough decency in me to not want my daughter to grow up around whores and drunks.' She broke off, still troubled by her decision and then said: 'My ex-husband, on the other hand, had the perfect environment. He was rich and powerful, owned this big ranch and was devoted to the child. He also promised me that he'd never reveal the truth to anyone, especially our daughter. He'd just say that her mother died and leave it at that. Which, I got to admit, he did.'

'Then what was your problem?'

'My fear that . . . one day the child might wonder why there were no pictures of her mother or any other kind of proof that she ever existed. It was probably all in my head but I couldn't stop worrying about it. So I made my ex-husband hire a nanny who pretended to be her mother. Then, when I felt our daughter was old enough to handle it, I had him send the nanny away. She left suddenly, in the middle of the night, and in the morning he pretended that she'd died. Naturally, our daughter was devastated. She cried and cried for days. Then for some unknown reason, she began to get suspicious and wouldn't believe her mother was really dead. She asked so many questions that finally, to convince her as well as some of the doubters in town, I had her father pay for a mock funeral, including a graveside ceremony as they buried the empty coffin.'

Coop grunted and slowly shook his head.

'I know, I know,' Lorna said, misunderstanding his reaction. 'Seems like a lot of trouble, just to make sure my daughter never knew I was her mother. But — '

'That ain't what I was thinking,' Coop said.

'No?' Lorna said, curious. 'What, then?'

'I was wondering how many other lies you've told me.'

'Why should I lie about anything else?' she said indignantly.

'Good question.'

'Are you referring to something specific?'

'Is gold specific enough for you?'

'Gold?'

'Yeah. A shipment of it that was supposedly on a train Gospel and I robbed.'

'You mean the Gold Train out of El Paso?'

'Exactly. Except it wasn't the real Gold Train and it wasn't carrying any gold.'

Lorna looked puzzled. 'Why should that involve me? I didn't tell you to rob it.'

'Not directly, no. But listening to you just now, it suddenly hit me. Del Gardo may have been the one who told us to rob the train, but, like everything else you just talked about, those orders came from you.'

'That's ridiculous! Why the devil would you think that?'

'Because I've seen Del Gardo several times since the robbery and not once has he asked me about there being no gold on the train. Don't you think that's odd? I mean, if I hired men to rob a gold train and they returned empty-handed, I'd be hammering on them until they either admitted they were lying or turned over the gold. But not Del Gardo, hell, he's never said a goddamned word. I kept expecting him to, and when he didn't, I figured he was waiting for the right time to come down hard on me. But that never happened. And now that I know how you played him, I reckon I know why: the robbery was just a diversion to keep the soldiers busy while some of your other men robbed the real Gold Train that was still in El Paso.'

'That's ridiculous!'

'Is it?'

'Of course! How the devil would you know about a robbery that did or didn't take place in El Paso?'

'Because I checked at the telegraph office, knowing a robbery that important would light up the wires. And sure enough, the next day news of the Gold Train robbery came click-clacking over the telegraph.'

Lorna stared long and hard at Coop. 'I was right about you all along,' she said finally. 'You're smart. Much smarter than you let on to other folks.'

'I try, as you once said.'

'And like you told me: you succeed.' She paused as outside, a buckboard pulled up before the house. They both looked out the window and saw Del Gardo help Gabriela to step down.

'Well, well,' Lorna said. 'Speak of the devil.'

37

Coop, surprised to see Gabriela and her father at Lorna's ranch, remained calmly seated at the bar while Lorna opened the front door.

'This is a surprise,' she said, trying to hide her uneasiness. 'What brings you two out here?'

'I don't know, Miss Lorna,' Gabriela replied. 'Papa wouldn't tell me.'

'Well, Edwin?'

'Invite us in and I'll tell you,' Del Gardo said gruffly.

'By all means,' Lorna said. 'Come in, come in.'

Del Gardo followed his daughter into the house, both surprised as they saw Coop.

'*Que es esto?*' Del Gardo demanded. 'Why are you here, *Senor* Coop?'

'For the same reason you are, most likely.'

Gabriela, who'd been jealously eyeing Lorna, said to Coop: 'I didn't know you two knew each other.'

'It's a small town,' he said affably.

'Now it's your turn,' Lorna told Del Gardo. 'Why are *you* here, Edwin?'

Del Gardo took a deep breath, steadied himself, said: 'It's time you told Gabriela the truth.'

Lorna frowned uneasily. 'About what?'

'That you're her mother. Please don't deny it,' he said as Lorna started to protest. 'This charade has gone on long enough. *Too* long in fact. And I want it to end right here and now.'

Gabriela and Lorna locked gazes.

'Are y-you?' Gabriela asked, nervously biting her lip. 'Please tell me the truth,' she added when Lorna looked away. 'Don't you think by now I deserve it?'

Lorna sighed and slowly nodded. 'Yes,' she said, facing Gabriela. 'You surely do.' She fell silent as she dug painfully deep into the past. Then she said firmly: 'The answer is yes. I am your mother.'

Tears flooded Gabriela's eyes. 'W-Why

didn't you tell me before? I mean, what did I do wrong that made you hate me so much?'

'Hate you?' Lorna exclaimed. 'Oh, precious, I didn't hate you! Not once. Not ever! What on earth gave you that idea?'

'What other reason would make you hide the truth from me, your own flesh and blood?'

Lorna looked at Del Gardo as if she truly hated him. 'That's a very good question, Gabriela. One, I'm ashamed to say, I have no real answer for. Other than the fact that, maybe — and this is no excuse — I thought you deserved better than me for a mother. I mean, think of who I was: a common whore, pleasuring men for eating money, who by chance bedded your father and gave birth to his seed, only to end up running a brothel above a saloon.'

Gabriela, mind racing, said: 'What about my sisters? Are you their mother too?'

'No, she isn't,' broke in Del Gardo.

'Their mother died, as you well know.'

Gabriela glared at her father. 'How would I know, papa? All I know is what you told me — most of which has been lies. So why should I believe this lie any more than all your other lies?' Before her father could reply, she turned to Coop, said accusingly: 'You might've told me.'

'Told you what?'

'That you were sharing Miss Lorna's bed.'

Her accusation cut deep. At the same time, Coop suddenly realized it was a way out of a relationship that he knew, for Gabriela's sake he had to end.

'I didn't figure it was any of your business.'

'You didn't?' she said incredulously. 'Not after telling me how much you cared for me? And knowing how much you meant to me?'

'Gabriela,' he said, heartlessly, 'I hate to tell you this, but as you get older you'll find out that most men will say just about anything to bed a pretty girl.'

'I'm afraid that's the truth,' Lorna chimed in. 'Like he says: most men are rats.' Turning to Coop, she added: 'Weren't you just about to ride off?'

'Yeah,' Coop said, taking the hint. 'Indeed I was.' He tipped his hat politely to Gabriela, the pain of hurting her tearing his guts apart, then nodded to her father, who ignored him, and walked out.

Gabriela tried not to break down, but it was hopeless. Bursting into tears, she ran into Lorna's bedroom and slammed the door.

Lorna eyed Del Gardo sourly. 'Was this really necessary, Edwin?'

'It was either this or watching my daughter — the love of my life — run off with a no-good drifter.'

Lorna considered his selfish excuse and then looked at her bedroom, from which came heart-broken sobbing.

'I hope Gabriela eventually learns to understand that,' she said, doubtfully. 'Otherwise, our little girl's in for a long stretch of misery.'

38

Outside in the broiling heat, Coop untied the buckskin and swung up into the saddle. Other than when he'd lost his wife, he couldn't remember ever feeling so low.

Overhead the sun, as if ashamed to shine on him, hid behind the clouds, turning the sky dark.

'Thanks,' Coop growled. 'Right when I need a rainbow, you run out on me.'

He tapped the buckskin with his spurs. The ornery horse took its customary swipe at Coop's foot.

Coop, his mind still on Gabriela, was slow to react. And before he could pull his foot out of the stirrup, the buckskin nipped the toe of Coop's boot.

The bite hurt like hell and Coop angrily punched the horse on the neck. 'Damn you!' he cursed. 'Now I'm really going to sell you for dog meat . . . ' His voice trailed off and it was obvious his heart wasn't into their on-going battle of wills.

The buckskin, feeling cheated, retaliated by breaking into a jolting, punishing trot that jarred Coop's bones.

With Ben Bridges:
THREE RIDE AGAIN
SHADOW HORSE
THE OKLAHOMBRES
THE PLAINSMAN